SUGARCANE

Cassandra Celia

SUGARCANE

CASSANDRA CELIA

SUGARCANE

First Edition | Publication Date: March 28th, 2023

ISBN-13 (Paperback): 979-8-9858659-5-0

ASIN (EBook): B0BVJR9BQK

Cover Design © Ria @graphicescapest

Article Images © Pia @crimsonsdesigns

Edited by Alexis Aumagamanaia @littlelionslibrary

Interior Formatting by Cassandra Celia @authorcassandracelia

Contents

ALSO BY CASSANDRA CELIA vii
CAUTION! ix

2 MONTHS AGO 1
PRESENT DAY 3
4 YEARS AGO 13
PRESENT DAY 31
2 YEARS AGO 39
PRESENT DAY 49
3 YEARS AGO 57
PRESENT DAY 63
11 YEARS AGO 69
PRESENT DAY 77
2 YEARS AGO 83
PRESENT DAY 93
1 YEAR AGO 101
PRESENT DAY 109
6 MONTHS AGO 113
PRESENT DAY 123
12 YEARS AGO 129
PRESENT DAY 139

PLAYLIST 147
ACKNOWLEDGMENTS 149
ABOUT THE AUTHOR 153

ALSO BY CASSANDRA CELIA

Stars and Other Monsters

The Elric Undoing

CAUTION!

By reading past this point, you are recognizing that SUGARCANE is an adult book that features mature and at times triggering themes and material. For a complete list of relevant content warnings, please visit my landing page located at the end of this book.

We are all in control of our own content consumption.

Thank you, and I hope you enjoy!

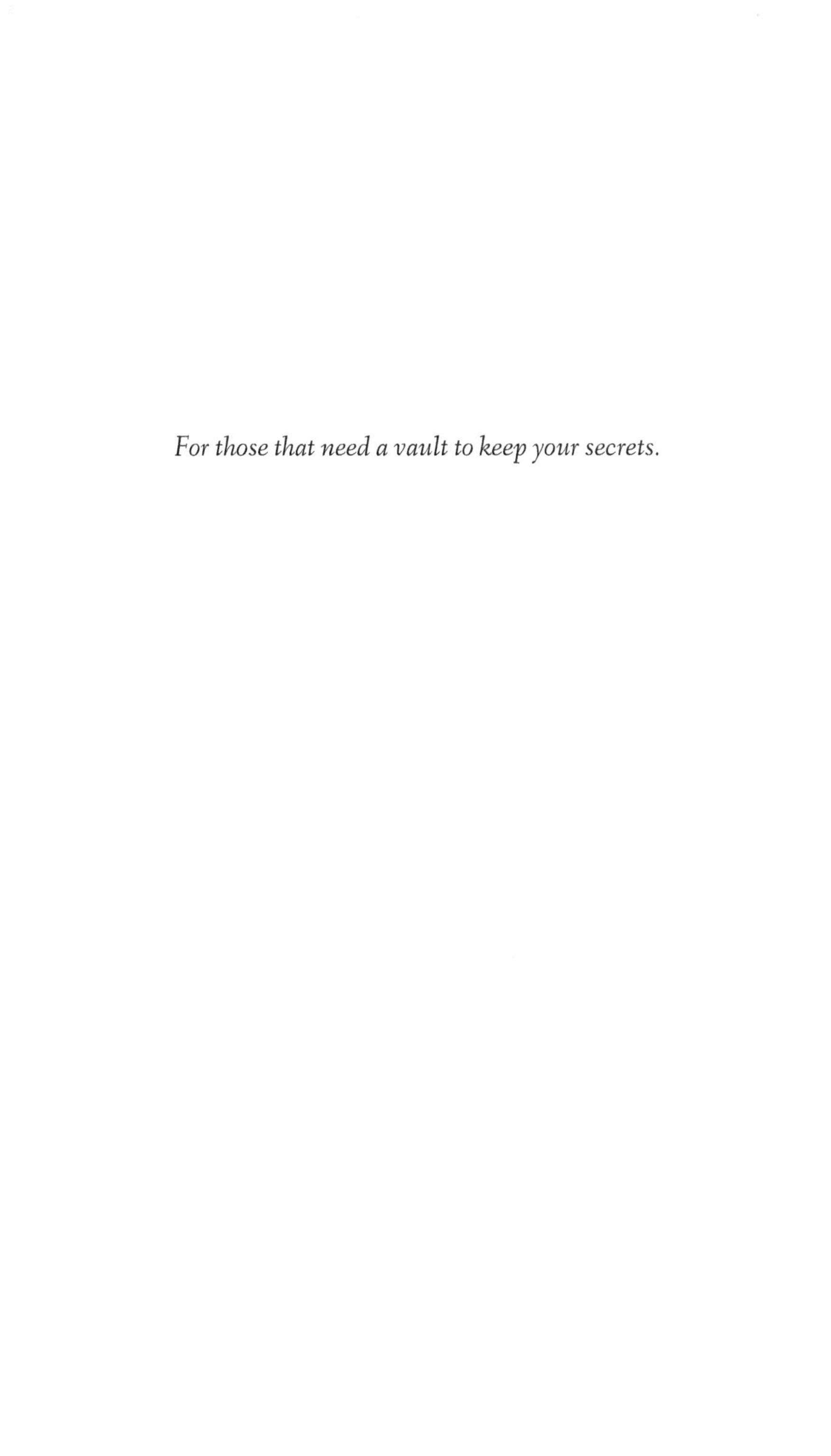

For those that need a vault to keep your secrets.

Vol. 25

[REDACTED] News

Daily Repor

WOMAN DISAPPEARS FROM LOCAL BAR

By: Anna Conroy

Hennesy Greene, 31, vanished in the early morning hours of Tuesday, September 4th, after leaving a local lounge and restaurant in [redacted]—about 50 miles northwest of [redacted]. Investigators say Greene left the local establishment at around 2 a.m., taking her bag, cell phone, and belongings with her. No cameras captured Greene exiting, though bar staff and patrons witnessed her speaking with a man before leaving on her own.

Greene last notified her family of her whereabouts at midnight but has since not responded to any messages.

Her car was located just a mile from the lounge, and her phone was turned off.

Family members filed a missing persons case just three days later. Police currently have no person of interest in the case.

"She always calls"

Greene's mother, Juniper Greene, 56, said to reporters, "Henn never goes anywhere without letting us know where she's going."

Missing person Greene seen here with her husband

Local Restaurant Greene was last seen

The [redacted] Police Department has asked the public to share any information that could help them find the missing woman using the hotline number listed below.

1-800-444-

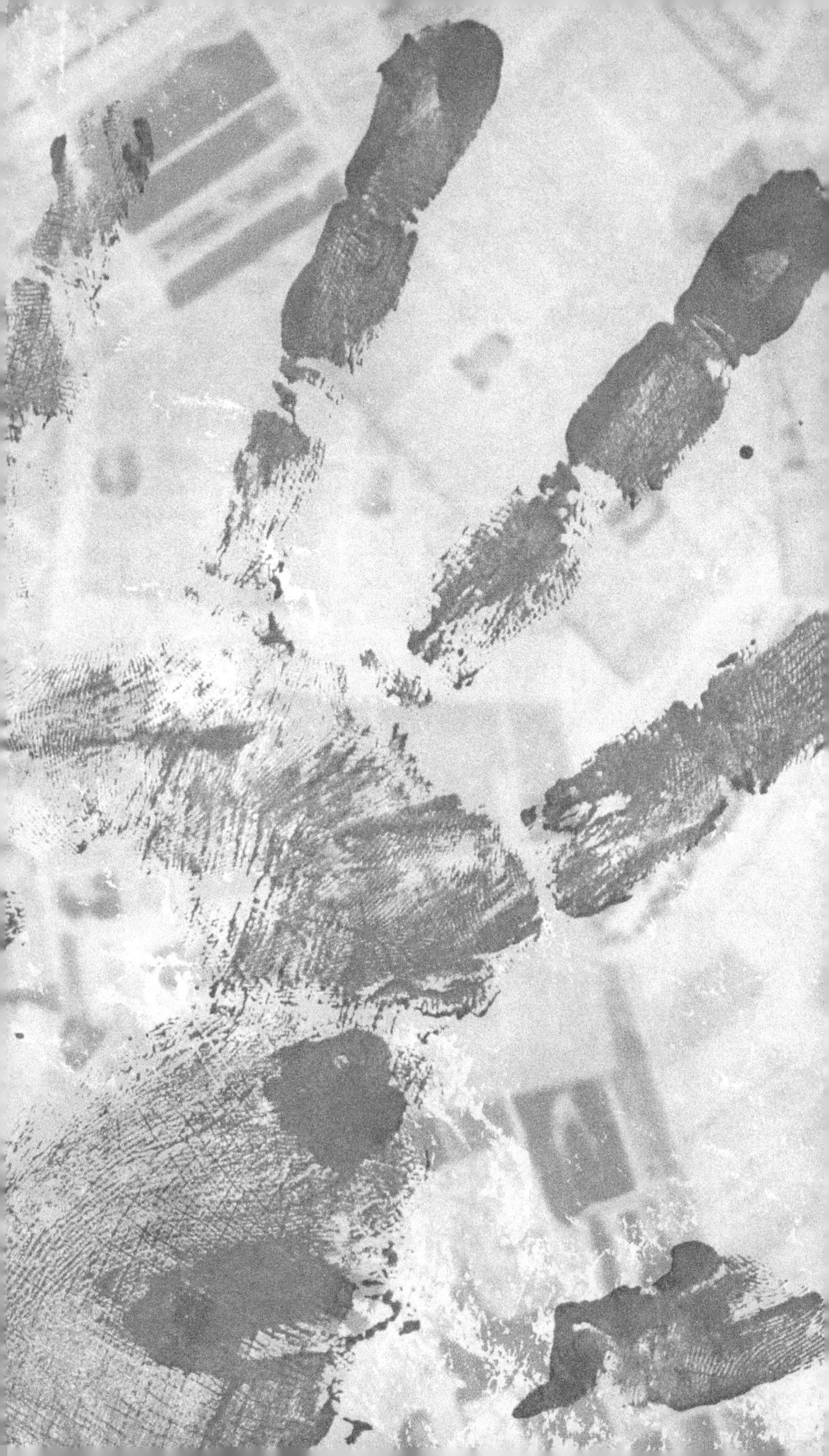

2 MONTHS AGO

I CRUMPLED THE NEWSPAPER IN ONE HAND AND slammed it down on the countertop, my lip curling into a dangerous snarl.

God fucking damn it, Caine!

PRESENT DAY

I THINK I MARRIED THE DEVIL.

Actually, I was sure of it. I had so much time to think about it down here in our unfinished basement, strapped to one of our dining room chairs, the putrid scent of the mold he'd promised to get rid of filling my nostrils. I was staring right at it, the soaking green and blue dots peppering the floor next to the utility sink. I would've handled it myself, but Caine kept me from it. He'd told me that women didn't do the dirty work, assured me it was a man's problem, and that he'd take care of it—that was five years ago.

I knew he was full of shit. I think I knew, even then, even before I *knew*, that he was hiding something from me down here in the basement. Something more than just old, rotted mold.

"I married the *fucking* devil," I whispered my thoughts out loud, almost smiling as the words blew past my lips.

And then I said it again, louder this time, *wanting* him to hear me. I wanted the words to be perfect, punctuated just as they needed to be, but with the sock shoved between my teeth they sounded a little worse for wear. It was a muffled "I ma-r da' u-ki' de-il." Not so threatening, or satisfying. And certainly not loud enough to rush him back down here.

Doesn't matter, it felt good saying it regardless. The words pressed against the back of my lips with familiarity, wanting to spill through them again and again.

I didn't believe in heaven or hell, or religion for that matter; *The Devil* was less of an entity and more of a concept. The word was able to encompass many things, all of which Caine personified. And so, it was often that I'd refer to him as such. To myself, obviously, in confidence.

Thank God he was upstairs with the door shut behind him. Caine liked to take his time with his *projects*. Sometimes, hours or days would pass between his shifts down here. I thought it was to keep me unsuspecting, but the longer I sat here, the more I wondered if it was because he needed to take breaks from the bloodshed himself. It was possible that Caine, *my Caine*, was not the monster I was making up in my head.

Then I remembered, once again, that I was strapped down against my will, awaiting his next move. I struggled against the ropes, wincing as they cut deeper into my arms.

What the fuck was wrong with me? Of course he was a monster. I needed to stop letting my emotions get the best of me.

I knew the minute this room went "under renovation" that he was, ultimately, preparing for me. I convinced myself that it was for his victims instead, and that by being his wife, I was excluded from his deadly activities. You could say my absence of self-preservation was crippling. I gaslit myself into thinking he would never come for me.

And, yet, here I was.

If only he'd get his head out of his ass, he'd know how

long I'd been covering for him and would understand that I wasn't stupid enough to scream or call the police. I could have done that a long time ago. He didn't have to gag me.

Hours of sitting down here did at least give me time to construct a plan. When he came back here, ready to do only God knows what, I'd convince him I was useful, and had been for a very long time. I was an irreplaceable tool within his arsenal. I would never say a word and let this fall behind us, never to be spoken of again if only he just *let me go*. I would sit down here for days if it would aid my case, so long as he blinded me and got rid of the gag that made me want to die every time I tried to take a breath or swallow.

Blindness, I could handle, but the fucking *mold*. It sat there, untouched, taunting me. He could have at least turned me away from it, but I think he knew how much it would bother me. And so I sat with my hands and wrists tied to the chair facing away from the staircase that led to freedom, my mouth gagged, and my eyes left perfectly untouched. The sink in front of me kept up its steady dripping, the mold seeming to grow larger with each passing second.

Devil.

I watched as tiny droplets of rainwater trickled down the wall behind the sink, puddling underneath. The sight of it was almost worse than the taste of his sock, the rust of his sweat a sweet tang in my mouth that I was certain I would never outrun. It would be a permanent aftertaste of anything I ate from here on.

I closed my eyes and breathed deeply through my nose, hoping that overindulging would get me used to it. Instead, my gag reflexes triggered, my throat clenching and unclenching in an open threat. My eyes widened in sudden fear.

Could I choke on my own vomit like this?

Fuck, it might be worth it to find out.

He wouldn't be able to hear me die if I went that way, which I knew would piss him off. With nothing but the rivulets of water and my own thoughts to keep me occupied, I'd go clinically insane in under a week, so maybe dying wouldn't be the worst thing that could happen. I was going to die anyway. At least then, it would be on my terms.

Of the ten years that Caine and I had been married, seven years were really good ones. They were so good that I had no doubts when he wanted to buy a home for us. It seemed like the most natural, next step we could take. And by God, I loved how my name looked next to his on the closing paperwork.

Caine's one requirement was a basement—in hindsight I should have analyzed that request—but at the time it was an easy compromise. His insistence was what kept us searching until we found this one. As I promised, the basement of this home became his continued *project*. In his own terms, it was "under renovations". How long renovations had been taking, four years to be exact, became an inside joke for us and even still, I smiled at those early conversations. Weird to know that the joke hid something more sinister than easy banter.

It was his hobby—obsession really—and he spent every waking moment down here when he wasn't working. You couldn't tell it had ever been worked on, judging by the lack of finished drywall and piles of materials that still haunted the corners in the back of the room. I could count on one hand the number of times I physically walked down here since we purchased the house, though. I wasn't the sort that checked in on Caine. It wasn't 'women's work', after all. And, I liked our easy joking too much to look too far into it.

We had a full year in our home, unscathed, before I realized that his *projects* included the killing and dismemberment of over thirty women. I don't think I understood it fully at first, but once I had, the full weight of my realization sent me spiraling into a quick burning rage. That bastard ruined our perfect family illusion, and I hated him for it. Every part of me ached for the *us* that I lost.

At first, it was the newspapers. I wasn't a reader, but it was hard to ignore the neighbors gossip when women started disappearing in a town this small. I think that was the first time I ever regretted Caine convincing me that this house was *the one*, and not the smaller ranch style home out in the country that reminded me of my parents' house.

Even with Caine right next to me, I needed to protect myself, like any other woman would. I started getting the newspapers delivered to read on my own, and kept up with the disappearances. At first they were seemingly isolated incidents, and then women started vanishing every month. One was kidnapped while walking her dog, another from a playground with her seven-year-old son.

Caine's work nights went longer and later in the evening, and when he slipped inside our house far past midnight, I was curled up in layers of sheets praying that I wouldn't be next.

He started getting sloppier.

He put a lock on the basement I never went into anyway, he had terrible excuses for coming home so late. A normal wife might have accused him of cheating, but Caine loved me too much for that. The thought never crossed my mind.

I don't know why my head went straight to his involvement, but it seemed like a more reasonable explanation than infidelity. For a while, the realization allowed me to sleep clearer because I knew it wouldn't be me—could never be me. Our love was far more important than whatever urges he felt.

And then it started pissing me off. My husband couldn't do the one thing that had been required of him; cleaning up his fucking messes.

My hands were starting to ache from the tension in the ropes. I'd asked him to tie it comfortably, not loose enough that I could get away, but not so tight that it would cut off all circulation. It was safe to say that he didn't listen to me.

The first hour was the worst. Pain echoed in my hands, and an unbearable panic settled in my chest. As if on their own volition, my fingers tugged and poked at the bindings to try to find a way to escape the hurt that pounded with each beat of my rapid heart. I couldn't see the tips of my fingers, but felt their rawness as the friction from the cords scrubbed skin away from muscle. Soon after—though I wasn't sure at what hour that happened—the pain and the panic subsided. And while it might have felt like relief, I knew that if I stayed like this for too much longer they would be limp and useless. It would be as if I didn't have hands; they'd be better off sawed from my body. At some point I stopped trying to tear at the ropes. The feeling that had gone from pain to numbness now felt like two bits of rubber grating against one another.

It had been about six hours, and I hadn't seen him since

he dragged the heavy dining chair down the stone stairs and sat my ass right in it.

He wasn't always like this. There were too many good moments in our life together. Dogs liked him, my friends liked him. Everyone I knew was drawn to Caine like he was a magnet, myself included. He had no red flags; he was quiet, maybe, but being quiet doesn't make you a killer. Everything I was taught to see as good and strong and important in a partner fell apart. My intuition failed me, my teachers failed me.

Everyone failed me.

In the early days of our marriage, Caine was sweet and gentle. He reminded me so much of my father—though, to be fair, my father was neither sweet nor gentle. It was more in the way Caine could see everything. He could see people, see through to their bones and to the core of who they were. His acute sense of observation made him stoic, a shadow against the walls of a crowded room. He wasn't intimidating, but might have been noted as shy by those that didn't know him as well as I did.

My father was the same way, sitting in corners and observing, never the center of attention, but always there.

He was consistent and accountable. All of that to say, he wasn't really a good guy either.

I gagged again, the smell of the mold and dust and... *wet* making bile rise slowly. I tried to swallow it back, refusing to let choking on my own vomit be the reason I died. I deserved something more vindicating.

The basement was getting dark, and by the limited view from the short window to my right I guessed that another hour had passed, just by the movement of light and shadows. I had no sense of time whatsoever, even with the ricochets of sunshine and darkness carpeting the basement floors. I could have been, and probably was, way off target.

I think it was the disappearance of daylight that beckoned him back here, all of his projects started after dark. I should have been paying more attention, I knew what was coming next.

Instead, I only listened to the threatening clicks of the locks as they sounded from behind me, the creaking of the door as it opened, and his heavy footsteps following suit. I cringed as the old metals on the hinges rubbed together, aggravating the air around it. It creaked and whistled even long after his body left the door frame. It was a warning, a song echoing through our home, singing melodies that welcomed Caine back to me.

4 YEARS AGO

Being a freshly married plaything all those years ago, friends and family told me that falling into a too-familiar routine would kill my marriage.

It never made sense to me—and honestly, I always thought that they were doing it all wrong if they really thought that. Routine is what I thrived on. I loved knowing that Caine would leave for work every morning at six. I loved knowing that he would be home every night by five. I loved knowing that he would make me dinner, we would eat and watch tv together, and we would go to bed. And then the next day, we'd start it all over again.

Routine did not kill marriages, people killed marriages.

Caine and I, in particular, loved our routine. I was thoroughly convinced that our marriage would survive simply because we chose each other—and chose our routine—every single day. We were comfortable, and I think that scared a lot of people. Big decisions were made on a whim, something that would make any other couple squirm. I remember sitting on the couch with him and watching some old rerun of a home improvement show. Caine and I both kept shouting at the screen and rolling our eyes.

We could do so much better than the hosts ever did, we thought. After an incredulous look at one another and a belly laugh that had us both sprawled out on the floor beside the couch, we decided to put that theory to the test. I was looking up listings and reaching out to realtors that evening.

We'd gone to several open houses and visited more homes in a week than I could count. In our search we both fell in love with the space this house offered—a sprawling Craftsman with three bedrooms, open windows that let the sunshine spill onto the hardwood, and a basement that seemed never-ending. The backyard was much the same—wild and overgrown, nearly two acres of woods stretching out behind the house. We'd viewed it in spring, when the light broke through the leaves and decorated the lawn with dancing shadows and a vision of the rest of our lives had hit me like a train. I could see Caine, sweaty and golden, pushing a lawnmower across the grass. I could see us, together, slow dancing in the kitchen, a pot of soup bubbling on the stove, falling snow piling up against the windowsill. If I squinted and tilted my head just right, I could see Caine in the yard with our children—maybe one or two, with his cola brown hair and my speckled hazel eyes, unruly and joyous, playing in the grass like they were the only people in the world. It was everything I had ever wanted, everything I had ever dreamed of.

Caine had made an offer before we even left the lot. That was our first *real* argument.

I had my sights set on another space further out in the country. It reminded me of where I grew up, with farms stretching for miles and chickens crossing the road. I wasn't really upset that he had gone and made an offer on the other house. He put illusions of happy children and irreplaceable memories in my head, made me so sick with *want* that I believed we would both die if we didn't get the Craftsman. But I was irritated and grumpy. It was the first time he had ever done something without asking me, and it came so naturally to him that I watched the seeds of doubt being planted in my head, breaking ground from the first desperate gulp of water.

When we left the showing, my eyes red from angry-crying, he looked at me with such youthful hopefulness that I was reminded of why I married him in the first place.

And by then, the argument was forgotten.

On the day we closed, he'd scooped me up into his arms and swept me across the threshold like we were a couple of newlyweds, our laughter filling the house and spilling from the windows. Two weeks later, he'd built me a greenhouse out back, knowing I couldn't keep a plant alive to save my life, for no reason other than I had asked and he could. Anything I wanted, I got. Caine knew how much that small ranch home meant to me, and I watched as his consistent and overbearing acts of kindness made me forget that the little house in the country ever existed in the first place.

I don't remember when it happened but, the Craftsman was the only place I could ever picture us in now. We built a routine, and it kept our marriage whole.

When Caine reminded me of my previous promise, and asked if he could start working in the basement to keep his fleeting hobbies contained, I easily agreed. I had no reason not to; I understood that we each needed a place to breathe and rest. He was down there every other day after that. I trusted him. We trusted each other.

That was what marriage was, in my opinion, and we did a pretty damn good job of it.

Tonight, he broke our routine. Instead of being home with me he was out at some hole in the wall bar, drinking with coworkers I heard so little about. I wasn't surprised that he said yes, I knew we both needed time on our own with friends. I *was* feeling slightly wounded, not only because he had ruined a night full of pre-planned movie-watching, but because I would have to go to bed alone, and he knew more than anyone how much I hated that.

My mother once told me that she'd rather be dead than be alone. She then gifted me that same fear. I hated being on my own. The silence was deafening, and there were moments where I was so consumed by intrusive thoughts that I couldn't breathe from the heavy weight of it. I would fill every lapse in conversation with a noise. Singing, humming, anything I could.

But I wouldn't call him, not yet. Even as the time crawled towards midnight, when I knew the bars would be closing soon, I trusted Caine to come back to me. Even if his absence was agonizing.

I showered in an effort to keep my mind busy. I washed my hair, rinsing and repeating until my hands were soggy and pruned. The skin wrinkled and folded, but I didn't care. I could spend hours under the water until I shriveled up like a day's old, rotten, dried fruit. The sound of running water was enough to curb my looming anxiety.

It burned my body like I was being consumed by fire, and though my skin blistered, I relished in it. It made every thought I had disappear, like dirty water escaping down the drain. As I melted under the weight of the boiling water, I could see myself starting to relax. My shoulders dropped away from my ears, the tension waning. I scrubbed my body with lavender infused soap, coloring my skin red as I rubbed it raw, hoping the essential oils would aid in my desperate attempt to wash away the stress my body was holding onto so tightly. I didn't want to leave the safety of the water, determined to stay standing here until the shower ran cold.

It wasn't until my skin was raw from scrubbing that I stepped out, dripping puddles onto the bath mat. Cool air hit every sensitive spot and I shivered as each step off the mat felt like stepping on ice. The tile defrosted under me, my puddles spreading across the floor like a flood, but I had no intention of grabbing a towel. I punished myself with nakedness, feeling more real and present than I had all night.

Any feeling was better than the stress of being alone. My attachment to Caine was bordering on unhealthy, but I couldn't help myself. I *wanted* him to go out, and I *wanted* him to make friends. But I also wanted him here with *me.* I was hopeless in the depths of my affection for my husband.

I dressed myself blindly, reaching around in the dark for whatever was softest, before rinsing away the last of my makeup at the sink. The wash rag, pulled from the top of a carefully arranged pyramid of rolled towels, was rough against my skin. I could feel it practically scrubbing the sins from my flesh as I dug it into the dips and folds of my face, ridding myself of the mask. It wasn't until I looked in the mirror that I realized I had grabbed an old concert t-shirt of Caine's, the constant reminder that he had such an unintentional pull on me. Our lives were entwined, even in the most mundane circumstances. He was mine, and I was his, and we were ours.

We were now tens of minutes past midnight, and I was eager to hold him again. He would come home to me, and I wouldn't have to worry about anything anymore, all traces of my previous anxieties gone.

Our bed was a welcomed relief in the midst of it all. I insisted on a queen size instead of a king when we moved in, wanting to feel Caine's warmth as we slept next to one another every night. It looked so large now, taking up practically half the room. The bed always looked so much bigger when there was no one in it. My eyes lingered on his side, the pang of his absence bouncing off of the walls of my ribcage. I breathed deeply, steading myself.

It was a mountain of white, our bed, all crisp sheets and a fluffy down comforter. I'd never been a fan of it. It was so impersonal. Caine had made the argument for neutrals, saying they required less upkeep to look nice. I had said that it felt like we were living in a hotel, our marriage housed in a liminal space meant for temporary comforts. It wasn't permanent, it wasn't our *home*.

If you asked me now, I couldn't tell you how Caine had won *that* debate, but he had and I'd slowly gotten used to the decor choices. There was something comforting in having a blank slate. It was like having a brand new canvas, waiting for a brush to sweep over it in the colors of our life. Everything was clean, and the scent of fresh linen mixed with mint filled the room. Despite its emptiness, I found myself smiling.

This was the routine I was craving so badly.

Sliding into my side of the bed was an immediate release of tension as my body seemed to dissolve underneath the comforter and deep into the crater I'd worn into the mattress over the years. I loved the feeling of cold sheets against my skin, and I buried my face into one of my pillows to inhale the sweet, sugary scents of old body washes and shampoos.

I didn't mind being alone when I was here like this, slipping in and out of consciousness, the familiar scents of home keeping me full. My goosebumps finally flattened across my skin, and my mind started to wander, dancing between worlds of slumber.

I would not call my husband, I would not count the minutes until he returned. I would lie in the deep cushions of my empty canvas and close my eyes...waiting until I could feel the warmth of my husband against my back again.

I would not sleep for long.

We lived in a quiet neighborhood, disrupted only by dogs barking in the distance.

Though I was used to the still nights from my parent's farm growing up, Caine hated it. We'd tried a noise machine for a while, but he hated that almost more than the silence, saying that falling asleep to whale sounds was something no normal person did, the rain was too fake, and white noise made him anxious. After some trial and error, and hundreds of dollars we'd never get back, we'd found out that simply turning on the fan was all he needed.

My priority had always been Caine's comfort above my own. So it was unlike me, to unknowingly choose this night to forget to turn it on. It was as if my body was preparing me for the horror I would come to endure. The fork in the road, the turning point in which my marriage would never be the same.

If the fan had been running, maybe I wouldn't have heard it.

The screaming.

It was jarring, the sound of a scream; a distinct shrill that sent fear straight through to my spine. It rattled my bones. Adrenaline shot through my body and I felt the pounding of blood rush filling my head. My body reacted instinctively, my back straightening until I was upright. I wiped away stray wisps of hair from my face, feeling the gross flakiness of dried drool on the corners of my cracked lips. I closed my eyes and fought against the blurriness at the seams of my vision.

My fuzzy surroundings amplified my fear, and I could hardly make out what was right in front of me, though my hand immediately went to pat the space next to me—Caine's still empty spot. My heart was in my throat, so high I felt like I was choking on it. I was too inexperienced for this, not near equipped enough to handle what a scream like that meant.

My bare feet touched the floor, my body falling out of the bed and onto all fours as if the perpetrator was inside my home—not outside in the darkness. Slowly, I inched my way to the window. I peeked over the windowsill, squinting my eyes against the fluorescent street lamps. The neighborhood was still, no movement or sense of awakening coming from the houses that surrounded us.

It was just one scream, but one was all it took. One that I could hear.

I thought I noticed Caine's car as I scanned our driveway. Relief coursed through my veins as my eyes confirmed that it was his. I couldn't see him, his big bulky shadow hidden from behind his headlights, but it *was* him.

He cut his lights soon after.

My intense relief turned to sudden shock, steeping with an overwhelming horror at what I saw as my vision finally cleared. I wiped at my brow and blinked several times before I had to cover my mouth with a soft hand, unable to tell if I was fighting back a scream or vomit.

He'd gotten out of his car so I could see him more clearly. He moved swiftly, far more gracefully than any man of his size should. I watched as he crouched by the driver's side door, crawling quickly towards the trunk. When Caine stopped and opened the backseat door, my entire body tightened.

He reached his hand inside, and what emerged must have been the source of the scream. There was nothing else that could have caused it, other than the sobbing woman at the end of his grip. Caine had fistfuls of sandy blonde hair that he pulled on roughly. I only caught glimpses of her through the tinted windows; the woman was thrashing against him, her hands wrapped around his wrist as she wept and kicked against the ground, fighting to get free. She tried to scream again, and I winced as if she had, but he shoved her head deep into the cushion of the backseat to stifle it.

Caine snarled into his open door, a face that seemed so wildly uncharacteristic of him that I couldn't help but think it was someone else. This wasn't the person I married, it couldn't be.

He whispered something in her ear and slapped her hard. I could feel it from where I kneeled, and physically recoiled from the impact. I shrunk from the window and scurried away, pushing and crawling and fighting to forget everything that was right in front of me. No other sound came. It was as if he turned her off, took away all the fight she had as he grabbed her from the car.

My body knew nothing but fear. I couldn't have been dreaming, my senses were too amplified for it to be nothing but a dream, but I was living in a nightmare. A nightmare I couldn't escape.

I knew they were coming here, where else would he go? Even if I could no longer see it, I *felt* it. I could feel it tugging on me now, tethering me to him. I watched him in the roll of film behind my eyes, playing out before me like I was watching a movie.

He pulled her from the back seat by the hair, dragged her across our lawn and up onto our porch. I winced at visions of her hair tangled in his fingers, the skin of her scalp pulling from her skull as he yanked her closer to him.

Caine fumbled for a moment when he stopped at the door, always forgetting which key was which. I felt his hesitation after each failed attempt, the woman attached to his hand squirming, kicking, flailing. The vision I'd put together in my mind—though erratic and ill-fitted it seemed—was the only indication that it was Caine and not an imposter.

I didn't hear him as he entered. I didn't hear the door open or the floorboards creak, he was as quiet as he's ever been. I yearned to go to him, and wanted Caine to convince me that I was dreaming; but I couldn't, because for the first time in my life, I was afraid of him.

I cowered.

I hid.

The basement door closed with an echoing *bang!* and sent my heart back into a frenzy. It beat so fast that I felt like I was going into shock. Each subsequent step down was accentuated by the sound of skin slapping against cement. My entire body recoiled, shrinking from the noise.

There were not enough tragedies in the world to outweigh the agony I felt. My breathing crumbled into dry heaves broken up only by the sound of my own wailing. I tried to swallow it back, tried to put a lid on my panic. I searched around desperately for my phone, careful to keep my steps light and my crying quiet as I looked. This was not Caine. This was not my husband.

Who the fuck was in my house?

I finally found it shoved under the folds of my sheets and scrambled to grab it, struggling to bypass the facial recognition password. It should have been easy at this point; call the police, send him away. *Protect the girl.* It should have been second nature.

Caine had a woman I couldn't name downstairs, and a deadly agenda I couldn't bear to conceptualize.

I tapped the screen, filling it with the numbers that promised safety.

9. 1. 1.

My thumb hovered over the call button, but I couldn't move. My fingers froze midair, and no amount of will or desire allowed them to move one more muscle. The numbers taunted me, screamed at me. They warned me of the danger I would put myself in if I didn't press that green button.

I couldn't do it. It was divine intervention, maybe, or just some sick delusion that kept me from saving her, from saving *myself.* I refused to believe it was happening, the harm he was causing, and I couldn't abandon him. Not yet.

Our routine meant more to me than her life, at that moment.

There was something more to this that I didn't understand. I convinced myself of that, and it was that lingering hesitancy that wouldn't allow me to call the police. It was the last strand of hope and delirium I had that kept me from doing the most rational thing I could do. What I *should* do.

Sometimes, love is not rational.

My legs stretched out from under me, creaking. I groaned in pain as the muscles tensed and prickled, pushing myself onto my feet, slowly and quietly, and wobbling as I straightened myself. I tossed my phone on top of the bed, leaving the promise of help behind as I snuck outside of our bedroom.

The house was as silent as my street, though it was, for the first time, unwelcomed. Each time the floors creaked under my weight I paused, worried that Caine could hear me. I watched in vivid daydreams of his calloused hands from years of hard work grabbing onto fists of my own hair. I watched as his face sneered, as he licked his lips in desire when he slammed my face against drywall. I watched as the person I loved didn't love me back, finding any piece of vulnerable skin he could to bruise and hurt.

I shook my head, trying to rid my mind of its horrible imagination. My path through the maze of our home continued despite my better judgment. I knew my destination, but my movements were slow, each step feeling forced. I couldn't stop, though, feeling the constant pull towards him, like our hearts were tied together on an invisible string.

To the basement.

Caine's *project*. The word suddenly held another meaning entirely. The doorknob shook under my fingers as I grasped it. I don't know why I left my phone upstairs, why I felt drawn to come down here. I was unarmed, barefoot, tear stained, with no motive other than to see with my own eyes that my husband was the monster my visions conjured for me.

I took one step down the stairs. Two steps. Three. Only a few slabs down I could feel tears welling at the creases of my eyes again, and there was nothing but that and the blood pulsing through my ears to keep me grounded. Caine's back was turned to me, and his hand was raised high in the air. It came down with a glorifying smack.

The sound of metal slicing through bone surrounded us all, causing my eyebrows to pinch together in a cringe.

Four steps. Five steps. Six.

I was halfway down the stairs now, my bare feet frozen from the cement that Caine kept promising to fix. Always promising, but never following through. The pads of my feet made no noise as I descended; my thighs were straining from how still I hovered, my knees bent and my stomach clenched so tightly that I was afraid my entire body could cramp at a moment's notice.

It wouldn't have even mattered if I stepped too loudly, or if the breath I had been holding slipped. Caine was too focused, his gaze only intended for the woman sitting in front of him. It was as if he had forgotten that I existed entirely. His world was empty of everything but the woman now strapped to a chair, and the sandbox of opportunity that laid before him.

He sawed his arm back and forth, and though I couldn't tell what was on the other end, the agonized wailing could give it away. The woman thrashed, though I could tell she was finally getting winded. Each scream was weaker than the last.

Caine laughed something wicked, a sound I wasn't familiar with. A sound that wasn't him. Not *my* Caine.

She was dying, right before my eyes, and my mouth was so dry that I felt as if my voice died alongside her. The woman moved as aggressively as she could, looking for a way out. Caine held onto her tightly, even as her head thrashed from side to side.

"Help me, help me," she whimpered.

My hand rushed to my mouth to quiet my breathing, to keep from making a sound, but I don't think it was enough. Maybe for Caine, but not for the woman with no name.

She looked right at me. I feared that she might have already been dead, eyes lolling and glazing over. But, as I stared into the pits of her irises, her moans came again. I'd recognized her desperate awareness then, and the girl looked at me as if I was her savior. Her eyes brightened, eyebrows arching and mouth opening to say something other than another scream.

I didn't know how to tell her that I couldn't be the hero, I couldn't save her. I couldn't do *anything*. Moments went by, the slick sound of Caine's metal slicing through more skin, more bone, more *her* in the still air. I think she understood then, who I was. How I couldn't, and wouldn't, save her. How in that moment, I was choosing *him*. I think it was that moment when she realized that it was the end, for her.

"HELP ME!" she screamed, looking at me with panicked dread. "HELP ME!"

Caine snarled and brought something heavy down onto her head. I heard the distinct crack of her skull as the reverberation ricocheted off the stone walls. It was a gross sound, the slick squishing of her insides enough to make my stomach curl.

Her screaming quieted until there was nothing left, and

I heard his mumbles of satisfaction as he watched the light leave her eyes. A flicker of rage filled my belly, to know that he was the last person she saw before she died instead of someone who loved her. It caused me to sit back onto my heels, to rock, to settle myself. It caused me to turn and run, to escape the evil this basement brought with it.

Because that's what it was, right? It was this place. This Craftsman. This basement. It couldn't be just Caine.

A piece of me died alongside her. That was it, the turning point. I knew that I had committed an evil that matched his. I was no longer good, or pure hearted. I was no longer a wife, but an accomplice to a murder. In a way, I felt my crimes were larger than his. I was the monster, because I could have stopped it.

I watched, and I did nothing. And, despite the fear that plagued me and the remorse that sat heavy in my stomach, I had done it to save *him*, instead.

I don't know how I made it back upstairs without him hearing me, I don't know how I would survive this. I shut the basement door quietly behind me as I climbed the stairs, and sprinted back to my room, to our bed.

The white sheets felt wrong. Though they had once given me a sense of security and safety, it felt less like the blank canvas I started with. I now envisioned pools of red, splotches of it painting the sheets, my consciousness, my innocence. An absolute, bloody mess.

I didn't make it before sickness spilled from my throat, covering the ground and the trash can closest to my night stand.

I rocked back and forth on the floor, pulling the covers from the bed over my head and trying to forget the fear in the girl's eyes. The girl who was most certainly dead, by the hands of my husband. It was difficult to separate my fears from reality. The sheets were not red like I had imagined, but still their stark white did nothing to comfort me. Instead it plagued me, taunted me. I had an open canvas, and I chose to tarnish it. Blood splattered across my vision, and, even when I closed my eyes, I couldn't escape it.

I couldn't tell how long it had been, me lying in my own vomit.

I vaguely remember hearing the guest bathroom shower running, and the slow heavy thuds as Caine moved his spoils from the basement up and through the front door. He never did return to bed, never checked on me in the night. If he had, he would have known. All too soon the light came slinking through my bedroom window. My eyes were caked with dried tears and snot. My nose crinkled from the stink. I didn't hear Caine any longer, but I was too afraid to look. He should be off to work. He was gone, away from whatever hell he inflicted, leaving me to burn in the catching fire.

But our routine still mattered.

My body was sore, and I climbed up onto the bed, reaching for my phone. My heart, still sunken in my chest, heaved as the numbers I'd dialed the night before burned bright like a beacon. The first of my own crimes. A reminder that I failed her.

I wasn't sure if I was blessed with a curse, or a miracle.

I quickly exited the call, several new notifications taking its place in succession.

CAINE

Got home late.

Slept on the couch.

I love you so much, and I can't wait to come home to you, Sugar.

His love enveloped me. Consumed me.

I put the phone in my waistband without responding. I moved as slow as a zombie, inching my way towards the bathroom to grab a towel. I wasn't worried about the noises anymore, no longer worried about being heard. Not in an empty house.

My head hung over the sink, cleaning the rest of the sick from my mouth, and soaking the towel. Soon after, I was scrubbing the floor, ridding the room of the last of my transgressions.

I should have gone to the authorities then. There was nothing to stop me, my husband was gone with no knowledge of my involvement. And yet, I didn't. I didn't want to, finding some self important reason to punish myself further. I would live with this, and hope it wouldn't happen again. I'd clean up this one mess, and let myself heal.

I couldn't lose Caine, the one I chose. The one that chose me.

This was nothing but another new routine.

My hand went to grab the phone from my waistband again, reopening Caine's messages when I finally trusted myself to respond.

See you soon, Candy Cane

PRESENT DAY

"Are you still alive down here?"

His raspy voice echoed off of the cement walls.

I kept my mouth shut.

He waited.

The silence stretched between us, broken only by the creaking of his steps down into the basement, the air heavy with the threat of him. A soft giggle came from the top of the steps, followed by a barked *ha!* that melted into a hiccuping guffaw. The sound drowned me, wrapped me up and dragged me down. I felt the urge to laugh—with him, at him, in spite of him—burning in my throat. I couldn't help it.

He'd always had the most contagious laugh.

In my seat I could picture the way his eyebrows raised, and how his eyes crinkled in the corners, more defined now than when we were kids. He seemed, on the surface, entirely harmless, his face, kindly and glowing, smooth from a fresh shave, did not indicate the monster that hid underneath. I could feel his presence as he honed in on me, his arms brushing past my shoulders as he approached me from behind. Our connection had always been electric. Even in a room full of people, I would know where he was, no matter what. I could feel my body respond to him being so close, and even strapped to the chair, my thighs pimpled with goosebumps. The hairs on the back of my neck raised in warning—or hunger—I couldn't tell which.

"I don't like you as much this way," he continued, knowing full well that my response hid at the back end of a crumpled old sock. His laughter settled into a humorous huff instead, "I crave your feistiness. It's endearing, though rousingly threatening. If there is anyone in this world that could rival me, it's you. I liked being challenged."

It was a very Caine response, and even in our respective positions, I was comforted by the familiarity of a conversation similar to this one that we'd had once before, a long time ago. At least some things never changed.

Caine's hand reached out and touched the soft side of my cheek.

His fingertips sent a jitter throughout my body, small shivers traveling up my arms. The need to move was unbearable, and my hands snapped against my bindings to relieve myself of the urge, coming up unfulfilled. A short winded noise escaped instead as the ropes burned into my arms and chest.

"Careful now, I don't want you to hurt yourself," he said, frowning as if he was genuinely concerned with my discomfort. I looked up, my breath catching in my throat at the sight of him.

Caine was as beautiful now as he'd always been. Hair that had always been cropped short now danced against his neck, the curls wild against his shoulders. I'd spent years trying to get him to grow it out, telling him to embrace the corkscrews that tumbled from his scalp, but he'd always fought me on it, saying it was too hard to manage and that it looked unprofessional. Clearly, his opinion had changed. As much as I hated to admit it, the length suited him. He looked like someone from the front cover of one of the romance novels you'd find on the nightstand at your grandmother's house—masculine and stern, handsome and wild. The frown he wore was a direct contrast from the wide toothy smile I'd grown used to, his hazel eyes burning with nothing but desire. I thought once that his eyes were meant for me, but truly that was how he always wore them. Caine was passionate about everything he did, and everyone he saw.

It was exhausting trying to keep up with him.

Looking at him now, I recognized the darker parts of him that I'd always ignored.

How his smile was more menacing than it was sweet, curling upwards only when he bested me.

How the passion and desire were saved for rough rounds in the bedroom or incredibly daunting feats of achievements—athletics, woodworking, and other hobbies he'd thrown himself into relentlessly. The rose colored glasses I'd worn in my youth were dulling, allowing me to see clearly what I was missing for so many years.

He was examining my wrists now, his thumb rubbing over bruised skin that the rope had rubbed raw. I could feel how calloused his fingertips had become, hard work etched on like a second layer. Still, my breathing was even through my nostrils. The moldy smell of the basement was mixing with the smell of his musky cologne that had stuck to his shirt for several days and sweat, and smelled just as the sock tasted, I concluded.

"You didn't try to free yourself," he noted, surprise coloring his tone, "I'm surprised."

He'd threatened to kill me on the spot if he saw me try to leave and he was surprised? There were no doors in the basement, and the one window I'd been watching earlier was smaller than the neighbor's feral cat. And storm-proofed. I'd be stupid to free myself, and he knew that. My eyes narrowed in his direction, taking note of the flash of disappointment that crossed his face.

Not even his beauty could distract me for long.

"Oh hush," he smiled at my scowl, reaching to tug the sock in my mouth gently.

"Promise me you won't scream?"

I didn't acknowledge him—my eyes were glazed over, watching every move he made while trying to control the ache in my throat. Honest to God, eyes really were the windows to the soul. Caine and I could have full conversations just by looks alone. He must have seen something he was looking for in there, because he reached for the sock again and pulled it free just seconds later.

"Sweet sugar, I missed you."

"Fuck you," I seethed.

His eyebrows lowered in shock, and I watched as rage spilled from him. His face turned a deep shade of red as heat filled his cheeks, and his teeth clenched so tight I worried he would chip a tooth. It was obviously not the answer he was looking for. A switch had flipped, and it was like he wasn't the Caine I remembered at all. This was someone else entirely. Just like that *first* night.

This was a killer taunting his prey.

Caine's eyes darkened, his tongue licking over his chapped, pouty lips. He raised his hand, and I didn't even flinch at the blow he landed across my face. I could feel his open palm before it connected with my skin, and as if I was a caricature from a cartoon, my head swung to the side, saliva flying from my mouth. The pain came after, my cheek burning with the imprint of his hand, my blood pounding in my ears.

Whiplash. And then, blood curdling rage.

He clicked his tongue against the roof of his mouth as he contemplated.

"Would you like to start over?"

I said nothing, and he raised his hand again in warning.

"Dulcie, babes, it's been over ten years, do you think it's the first time I've ever heard you tell me to go fuck myself?"

"It's the first time you hit me over it."

I think my voice startled him. Ever the narcissist, Caine took a step back, his hand lowering. We locked eyes again, a standoff. I begged him to hit me again, my eyebrow arching in challenge. Caine shook his head, and it was at that moment that I felt a surge of victory. He knew how much I wanted to make him into my father. It was the only way I could rationalize everything else; if he was as terrible to me as my father was to my mother.

"I-didn't—you made me do it," he said at last. Caine was a different sort of monster, and I knew—even without him telling me—that he would never be that kind of evil.

Somehow, it made me feel better.

"If you say so, Caine."

My answers were bothering him because they weren't what he wanted to hear. I could see his eyes shift to the ground, contemplating whether or not to shove that fucking sock halfway down my throat again. He said he wanted fire, so I would give it to him. I was

going to die here, anyway; I wanted to make this as hard on him as I possibly could.

His doting wife was a controlled flame, combative in only the ways that served him. He didn't want the real me—

I was no candle flame. I was a fucking wildfire waiting to burn the city down.

I could tell he was getting uncomfortable, he did that thing where he twisted his fingers through his belt loops and tightened his grip. With the immediate threat of his hand gone again, my body relaxed despite my better judgment.

"Dulce, what are we doing here?" There was a timidness in his voice, sounding so sincere that I almost believed that he was genuine. It was weird, to see this softness again after knowing he maimed too many other women in our home. It felt wrong on a level I couldn't quite articulate. This was no mask, but the person I lived with for ten years. A saint, an empathetic, kind man.

"Do you really want to have that conversation right now?" I asked, incredulous. He flinched away from my tone, pieces of the Caine I remembered coming home, just for a moment. Then he hardened, returning to the man that tied me to this chair. The man that was going to kill me, now.

"God you had so much potential," Caine whined, his hands untangling themselves from his belt and running through his thick waves of hair. He turned around and paced toward the wall. I watched the way his biceps flexed and the toned muscles running down his back tensed underneath his shirt. In no world could I overpower him.

"I must admit," he said with an uncharacteristic amount of shyness, tilting his head back in my direction. The switch flipped again, a big breath traveling from his belly to his chest, then out of his mouth on a long exhale. He rushed me, stopping just before he was close enough to kiss me. Caine reached his hand out to caress my cheek, rubbing harder at the bruises again. I hadn't noticed that my eyes had welled with tears until his hand pulled away from my face, wet and glistening.

He lifted his fingers to his mouth and tasted them.

"I changed my mind. I love seeing you this way," he continued, "Tied up. Ready for me to do whatever I want. I never thought it would bring me this much joy." I spit at his feet, still not wanting to dirty his beautiful face, no matter what he was doing to me. How sick and twisted was that?

"I thought you liked my fire. Isn't that what you just said?" I challenged. It wasn't so much a real question as it was sarcasm. The look on Caine's face told me that he took it seriously, nonetheless. We both knew that we were stalling, both unwilling to make the next move. I never doubted that he loved me; he must still. Despite it all, Caine was trying to prolong our time together.

This night could only end one way.

"Oh, I do, I just didn't realize how satisfying it would be to see you in the same chair that so many of them sat in, too."

2 YEARS AGO

I SNAPPED MY GLOVES AGAINST MY WRIST AND WINCED against the bite of the rubber. It was a different type of hurt than what I was used to, but it was a welcome visitor— it was sharp and it stung like the snap of a rubber band, not like the dull ache of the last few years. It was good to feel something again, no matter how painful.

I couldn't remember what it was like when Caine and I were dating, when there was no pain at all. That was a long time ago, and the memories were fading day by day. I wondered if it was because of us, or if all marriages lost it. The spark. The love.

No, I didn't fall out of love with Caine. I still loved him so much that it was hard to breathe some days. My love morphed, though. Eight years in and it warped itself into something I couldn't recognize anymore. It was no longer an innocent love, but a messy one. Now I was stuck on my hands and knees, scrubbing at foot prints of dried blood— the ones he'd forgotten to wash away.

Everything hurt. From my knees against the hardwood

floor, to my arms as they scrubbed back and forth, to my heart that was broken.

I lost count of how many times I'd done this for him by now.

It was getting old, waking up day after day, not knowing if he had killed someone, or cleaned up his own mess. I never thought Caine was a dumb man, and I wondered again, not for the first time, if he knew that I was doing this for him. A test of sorts, to see how far my love would go. I was winning, if that was the case.

My hands were cramped, but the grime was finally starting to come up. I wiped a bead of sweat from my brow, scrunching my nose and narrowing my eyes as I picked up the rag. It was rust hued now, but the color stopped bothering me long ago.

I was no longer afraid of blood.

The house always vaguely smelled like bleach, but it had been that way since the day we got married. I think we just both really loved the smell of a crisp, clean home. As the thoughts peppered my mind, my hands followed suit. I picked up the bleach in question and poured another layer onto my floors.

Caine was good at hiding his indiscretions. He always cleaned up after himself, and any wife that paid less attention than I did wouldn't notice a thing. I always paid *too* much attention to Caine, though. My fault, really. He was good at scrubbing, but he never really got the corners right. The places you wouldn't think to look.

That was okay, because he had me. I just couldn't stand the thought of someone else's blood caking my home. Often I worried that maybe he *was* more careless than I believed. If he didn't have me, would someone notice? Could he lose everything if I didn't look after him just right? Did I even want to, anymore? It was beginning to feel like it was more tedious than it was worth. Because *no* other wife would do this, no other woman would give this man anymore rope than he deserved. I was giving too much.

It wasn't his best work, he didn't even think to go over it twice. Fucking *men*. I could still see the stark outline of the bottom of his boots, painted with dried red flecks. He'd rushed himself, and I wondered if he planned on getting to it later on his own, assuming I was too oblivious to notice it like the meek and docile wife that I was, or if he'd look at the work I'd done and think *he* did an excellent job. Probably the latter, cocky man.

I started to feel pride swell in my chest, despite the soreness in my forearms. Thoughts of Caine's carelessness were now long forgotten when I reminded myself that I was *good* at this. Whether he recognized me for my efforts was unimportant. I knew the sweat that went into this work, and that was enough for me.

As the tracks continued to lift from the ground, a wave of satisfaction flushed through me. Leaning forward with wafts of cleanliness infiltrating my nostrils, I breathed in deeply. The scent of my achievement was deliciously addicting.

I sat up on my knees, happy with the renewed state of our wooden floors and wiped the sweat that formed at my brow again. I was glad Caine had left for work already. He would be at the office for a few hours, and it would give me enough time to fix myself up and forget that last night had ever happened. I was starting to get good at forgetting all of the terrible things he did. And, by association, all of the terrible things I was doing, too.

I crumpled the dirty rag in my fist, and took a deep breath as I stood up.

There, good as new.

His haphazard, amateur work never improved, but mine did. It was the only reason he hadn't been caught, yet. We played this delicate game; I knew he didn't want me to know, and so I played the part. What was I going to do, send my husband, the love of my life, to jail? Whatever the game was, *I* was the winner. I suppose I was also the loser, but I tried not to worry over that part.

It was fucked up, I know. But I was a good person. Despite it all, I still believed that he was, too. Sometimes we can't control the demons that haunt us. When I married Caine, I vowed to him that I would be there, until death do us part. I planned on taking that vow as literally as I could.

He needed me, and it was that knowledge alone that curbed my fleeting rage.

I grabbed a spare plastic bag, one of the ones left over from a grocery trip last week, and stuffed the remnants of his latest project deep within its contents. Tying it up into the tightest knot I was able, the evidence swung from my grip as I walked towards the front door. It was cold outside, and as I watched the comfort of fall transition into winter I could feel goosebumps pepper along my skin. Early in the morning, everyone else had already gone to work, or slept in. I felt safe as I walked barefoot to the side of our home and dumped the plastic bag into the large can.

I wasn't worried that anyone would see me. And, if they did, they'd have nothing to be suspicious of either. We sat at the end of a dead-end road, with older neighbors that hardly gave us the time of day. No one would ever suspect us; we were the perfect, unassuming family. I didn't want to think about it too hard because, contrary to my own beliefs, I knew this made me a bad person.

"Your husband already gone for work, dear?"

I jumped, turning around to see our next-door neighbor smiling at me from over the hedge. So much for ignorant neighbors. I hadn't cared to learn more about her than her name, and didn't care to talk to her any more than I had to. Marge knew us though, to my disdain. She was a nice enough woman, but it'd be better for all of us if she kept her nose in her own property, and away from ours.

"Y-yeah" I stammered. I knew better than this, but at least she didn't seem suspicious. Why would she?

"He gets up so early, sometimes. I can see when the lights flicker on from your kitchen. I remember when Chuck used to be able to do that. Now we're a bunch of old-timers. Don't get up until long after the mid-morning news"

My heart skipped. Why was she looking in my kitchen window?

"You're up early today, then!" I laughed uncomfortably, lifting my hand to scratch at the back of my neck. Marge shook her head.

"Chuck snores so loud that I have to leave the bed sometimes. I fall asleep on the chair in the living room. Hurts my back and everything. The things we do for the people we love, right?" I looked around as Marge kept on talking. Something about the sentiment put me at ease. The moment of fear had passed, she wasn't the type to be sneaky. Marge was just a good neighbor.

"Let me know if you want me to pay for a hotel room for you," I joke, smiling at her for real this time and dismissing myself with a small wave.

"I might take you up on that!"

We shared another laugh and I tried to retreat back into my home.

"Dulcie!" I turned my head to see Marge still leaning

over my hedge. I didn't respond, keeping my face stoic as I waited.

"You tell that husband of yours thank you for me! He was such a doll and cleaned our gutters last week for us. Sweetest fellow, you certainly got lucky to have such a handy man around." She shook her head, a knowing smile falling from her lips like there was some inside joke between us. " I was hoping we could come over for dinner this week? Chuck and I can bring over our kid's favorite casserole dish, and of course we'd leave the leftovers for you. We miss our kids, and you guys remind us of them. It'd be a real treat, I think!"

Caine would have jumped the gun. Caine would have over-worried. Caine would have killed her for her questions without knowing her innocence.

I was smarter than that. He was lucky to have me.

"I-uh. We're busy this week, Marge. Got a lot going on with work and stuff. Caine is so tired when he comes home. Can we rain check?"

It broke my heart as I watched her face visibly fall. I hurt her feelings. Her kids moved across the country a few years ago with their own kids, and I don't think they visited often. I would have to remember to invite them over for dinner when I knew Caine was on his best behavior. This feeling sinking low into my gut felt worse than it had when I was scraping blood off the floor.

"That's fine, sweetie," her tone was visibly duller, and her voice cracked, "We know you both are busy bees! Just let us know when, okay?"

My returning smile didn't meet my eyes. "Of course. I'll talk to Caine about it."

She nodded and returned to her side of the yard, leaving behind nothing but small imprints in the brush. I felt awful, and retreated back to my home with my tail between my legs.

Once I was back inside I shut the door behind me, running my hands through my hair to release some of the built up tension. I pulled out my phone from my back pocket and dialed Caine.

"Sugar, what's up?" He answered on the first ring. Sometimes we go back to the place we used to be, where love was all that tied us together. I got glimpses of what we could have been, if he hadn't done what he did, and if I hadn't seen it. It all felt fake now, forced. Somewhere between him becoming the world's most dangerous killer and me being the world's most dutiful wife, we broke.

I knew it was the layers of secrets between us, but I would continue to ignore it as long as I could. I loved him, and he loved me. Love will be enough. It has to be.

"Dulcie, honey?"

"Sorry, Caine," I sighed. Just the sound of his voice put me more at ease. It relieved the remorse I felt after my conversation with Marge. "What's up?"

He let out an amused laugh. I loved the sound of it, his breath was light and airy and there was no hint at the horrors he committed last night. His shoulders didn't seem tense, his voice wasn't strained. Caine seemed oddly at ease. "You called me, doofus."

"Oh shit, that's right."

"Are you okay? Is something wrong?"

"No," I answered honestly. Nothing was wrong, in fact. It was a false alarm. We're still safe, you're still safe. But I couldn't say that out loud. "I just wanted to hear your voice."

I could practically see him smiling. I learned long ago that Caine loved to hear how much I loved him.

"What do you want?" His tone was playful and it made

my insides squirm. How is it that I still wanted him after all of the bad things he'd done?

"What? I can't tell my husband how sexy his voice is?"

Caine groaned. I can't remember the last time we had good sex.

"Sugar, I can't leave yet. They're making me stay a few hours." His voice turned husky. He'd go to the bathroom and jerk one out, he'd come home early despite this protest. We would have sex, but it would be a disappointment to us both. Things were just different after being married for eight years.

"When will you be home?"

"Probably around three or four. I can try to swing for earlier, but some of the guys that were supposed to be here for that job I told you about last week didn't show up. So we're scrambling to find some more, fast."

I grumbled, noting my own frustration. At least I could make sure I finished cleaning before he got back. It would be my good deed of the day.

I called Caine because I needed to remind myself that I wasn't doing this for nothing. It was a moment of weakness, but it did the job. I could feel my pulse slowing each passing second. I shook my head and I gathered myself.

"Dulcie, sugar?"

"Sorry! Okay, did you want anything for dinner?"

"Your idea of dinner is take out. Do you mean, what would *I* like to make for dinner?"

I was getting bad at this, I don't really know why. I had kept myself together for so long, and some of my cracks were starting to show.

"Heh, yeah, I guess you're right."

There was silence at the other end of the line.

"Babe, is everything okay?"

"Of course!"

I knew he wouldn't buy the sudden high pitch in my voice, so I tried to pivot; it was easier that way. "Actually, I was thinking..." I could hear shuffles of movement from his end of the line. Why had I called him? I was making a damn fool of myself.

"You always get into trouble when you think like that." I smiled, and warmth filled my cheeks. He wasn't wrong.

"I was thinking we should put up blinds in the kitchen window."

I could tell that I had confused him. All sounds of shuffling vanished, and I could practically hear the frown as he hummed. "Why?"

"I think I saw someone looking through them this morning. It could have been shadows, but you know we have the nosiest neighbors. What if I'd been naked? I'd just feel more comfortable with something covering them. I don't think the curtains are enough."

Silence followed. Had I gone too far? Did he suspect?

"I'll take care of it," he finally mumbled. There was nothing more than the low, heavy breathing on his end of the line. "Dulc, I got to go, the guys need me. I'll see you when I get home?"

I nodded, not saying anything before I hung up the phone.

What the fuck was wrong with me?

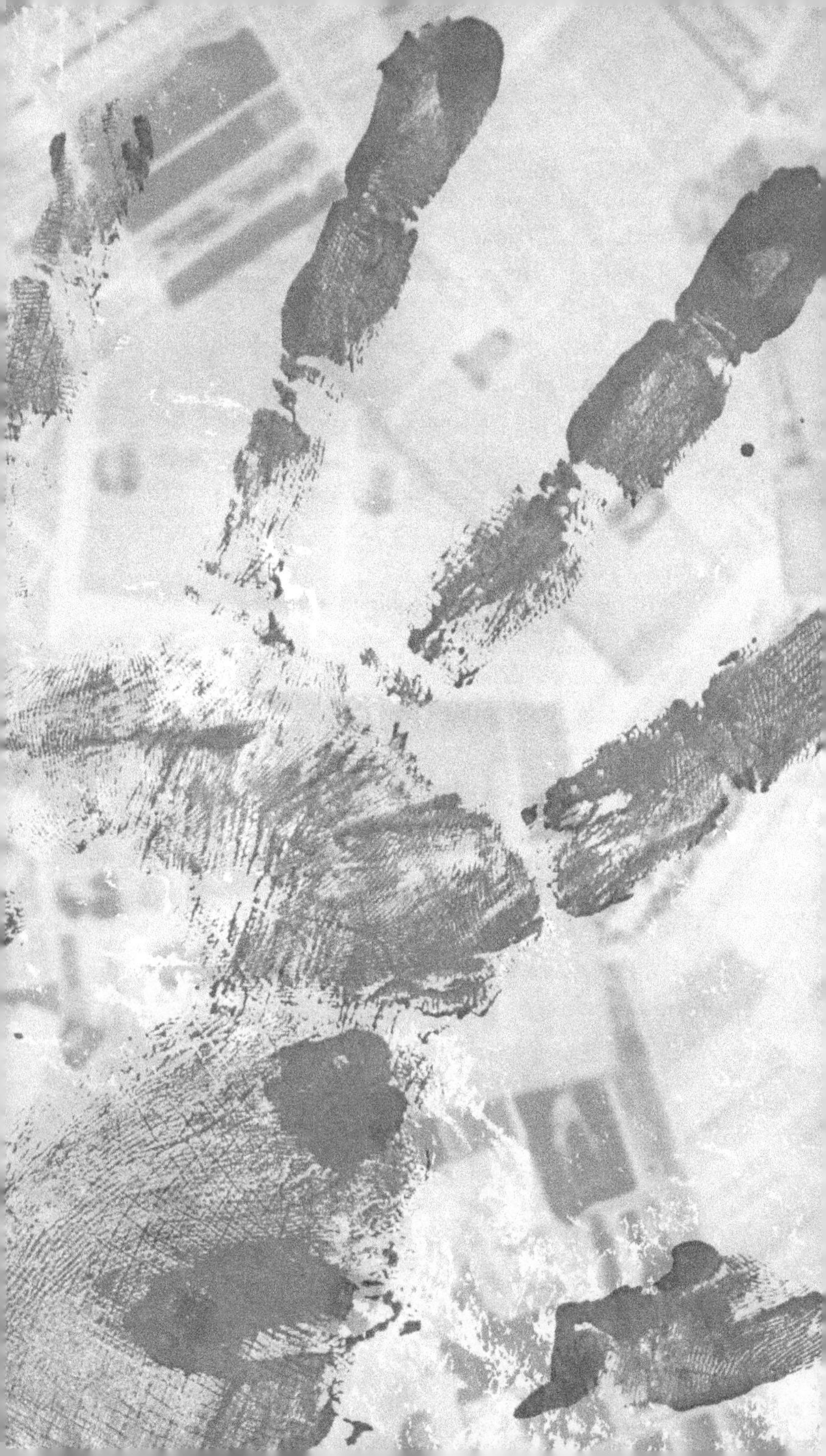

PRESENT DAY

"How many were there?" I whispered, not wanting the answer, but needing it.

"I don't think that's something that would do you any good knowing, Dulcie." He said with a sad smile. He was right, it would only make this harder. I almost loved the idea of him protecting me from it—the nightmares of his horrors and transgressions plagued my nights, and there were days when I couldn't think of anything else. Actually knowing would be torture.

Even if he didn't know what I had done for him these last few years, he always knew what I needed at that moment. A long, pregnant pause formed between us as he stared at me. He was waiting for something, though I couldn't tell you what he wanted. It was the first time in a long time that our nonverbal cues were lost in translation. There was something missing in those eyes of his, and I couldn't find my way back to him.

The prolonged gaze made me squirm, so I tried a different approach, instead.

"Where's your big knife? Your 'serial-killer-station'?" It

was meant to come off as a challenge, but the way my voice shook betrayed the fear hidden in the question. The bravado I'd felt vanished quickly, and I worried that before long I would fall into his trap again. A wildfire smothered by his wave.

Caine laughed again, the sound melodic against my eardrums. Fuck, I needed to get over his laugh. I blinked first, the battle lost, and he finally took a step away to walk toward his desk underneath the window; as if he was prompted by my question. Like it reminded him of something he had forgotten.

Daylight was just about gone now, nothing but the evening glow illuminating the basement. Caine's wrist raised to tug on the string attached to a lightbulb above his workstation, and the fluorescent yellow it emitted bounced off the stone walls. I could see him more clearly now, and I watched silently as he opened each drawer and cabinet, gathering different tools and materials I couldn't recognize from where I sat.

"You watch too much television. Remember when I told you it would rot your eyes?"

Caine chided me as if I were a child, but the sentiment was cloaked in a threaded smile. "Especially the news. You always were so invested. You shouldn't believe everything you hear, Dulcie."

The blade that glinted under the lightbulb was just a normal butcher knife. He grabbed it and lifted it to his face, admiring the shine. Caine turned around and leaned on his desk, sharpening the blade on something I couldn't see in his other hand.

"Authorities make things up all the time, Dulc," he continued, his gaze intent on ensuring the blade's sharpness, "They make up names and tell tales they don't have the full story to. I never understood why you just believed everything they told you."

He was talking to himself more than he was me, and I couldn't help but cringe as the sound of the blade skimming against stone made my insides fold.

Caine stopped suddenly. He looked at me intently, awaiting my answer, though I couldn't keep my eyes off the knife in his hands.

"I believe in evidence, Candy Cane." I replied with my eyes flicking to his face, hoping to jar him with casual use of our nicknames. It seemed to do the trick as his eyes widened significantly. Catching him off guard sent a surge of confidence through my bones.

"Sugar, you have a lot to learn." Caine's face dropped, contemplation flooding his features in earnest. He was always so easy to read, I thought. But then again, he kept himself hidden from the public eye for so long, I was starting to wonder what was true at all.

Caine circled me and my neck strained from trying to follow him in my periphery. I heard a clatter behind me as he discarded his blade sharpener, and the stone hitting concrete made me flush with a new wave of fear. My body iced, the hairs on my neck standing on end as he approached me from the side and pressed the cool of the blade against my arm. I jolted in my seat.

"So jumpy," he said, the huskiness of his voice deepening as amusement coated his expression. Caine rubbed the blade against my skin, keeping great care to not press too deep on the sharp end.

"Just fucking kill me, Caine,"

"I don't want to kill you, Dulc. Why would you even say that?"

He had the audacity to sound offended.

My eyebrow cocked, and despite my fear, I could feel a familiar eye-roll coming. I strained against the ropes again for emphasis. Caine noticed, and the shadows danced around his pupils.

"Sweet sugar, if I let you go, you're going to leave. And if you leave, you're going to the cops. I've come too far to let that happen. It's not like I want all of this. It's who I am, I can't help it."

"I asked you to kill me, not let me go," I snarled. He only shook his head again.

"I don't want to kill my wife, who was just at the wrong place at the wrong time. You see my predicament?"

If only he knew just how long I covered for him. How with each project and each evening he dragged pieces of a corpse to the trunk of his car, I made excuses to the neighbors. I turned a blind eye.

"I. Won't. Tell." I ground out, punctuating each word slowly, "If you won't kill me, let me go, we can talk about it. Caine, we can fix this."

"They always say that," Caine mused, idly twirling the knife in his hand, "What makes you any different?"

"I am your *wife*." I echoed his earlier phrasing. Maybe hearing it enough would help him realize that I could be on his side. That I have been on his side this whole time. It was the simple truth of it. I loved him too much. I let him get away with terrible, awful things because I loved him.

Caine thought about that for a moment and hummed. The blade in his hand moved high enough that it was now in my direct line of sight. Caine shifted in front of me again, dropping to his knees. Even on his knees, his face was still close to mine, only the butcher knife separating us.

"Why did you have to see me?" He whispered, closing his eyes. It was so low that I could barely hear him. He ran the knife down the bridge of my nose, and I winced as it left a trail of blood in its wake. His voice was quivering, and I almost believed him when he said he didn't want to kill me after all. A small whine left my lips, but he didn't seem to hear it.

"You weren't careful enough," I answered him honestly in a quiet voice.

And God I wished he was.

I opened my mouth to confess, to tell him that it wasn't the first time I'd tried to help him. It wasn't the first time I covered his shortcomings.

His sins were as much my own, and even if it would kill me, I needed him to know. I loved him—no, *love* him. I protected him. I hadn't let so much as a word leave my mouth before the knife suddenly sliced down my nose and straight through my lips. They split open, and blood cascaded down my shirt. Caine jumped back in surprise from his actions, his eyes flicking back and forth from the knife in his hand, to me and my now open wound.

Shooting pain rushed through me and I thrashed against the ropes, wanting desperately to free myself and caress my mouth, where my teeth were starting to stain ruby red. Sensing my panic, Caine moved the butcher knife to cut at the ropes, and once I was free I fell to the ground, sore arms raised to cover my face. My pain overcame his desire, and for a moment he was simply my husband again, and not my captor.

"I'm sorry!" He screamed, frenzy making him drop his knife as he crouched next to me.

Caine touched my hair and my arms, his hands rubbed circles into my back. "This wasn't supposed to happen this way, I don't know how to stop it!"

"Get the fuck away from me!" I screamed at him, my

voice sounding hoarse from the overexertion. *Fuck him!* Fuck everything he was, and everything he did. He didn't deserve to know, and I could never let him win. How could I be so stupid?

He scrambled to get up, leaving his butcher knife where it lay as he ran up the stone steps. I heard the door shut behind him, the lock clicking into place, and then silence surrounded me.

When he was gone, when the rhythmic sounds of him pacing above me were consistent thumps across the ceiling, I moved.

First, my head, which roared with agony.

Then, my mouth, which caused a sharp cry to leave me as I swallowed. My lips flopped around like useless pieces of flesh, hanging from my mouth with no support. I made no more effort to speak, fearing the loss of them completely.

Finally, I pushed myself up, my muscles straining as they hoisted my body weight up and off the ground. Once I was sitting upright, I wiped at my eyes and I tested opening them again.

Everything blurred at the edges, but I couldn't waste much time.

Tiny pinpricks cascaded through my body, blood flow finding its way back to my legs even as it streamed from my face. My joints cracked and popped as I tried to stand, and I stumbled as I regained my footing. Caine's pacing continued upstairs, and it was the only indication that I was safe, at least for now.

I glanced around me frantically, reaching for the butcher knife he left discarded on the ground.

His regret will be the end of him.

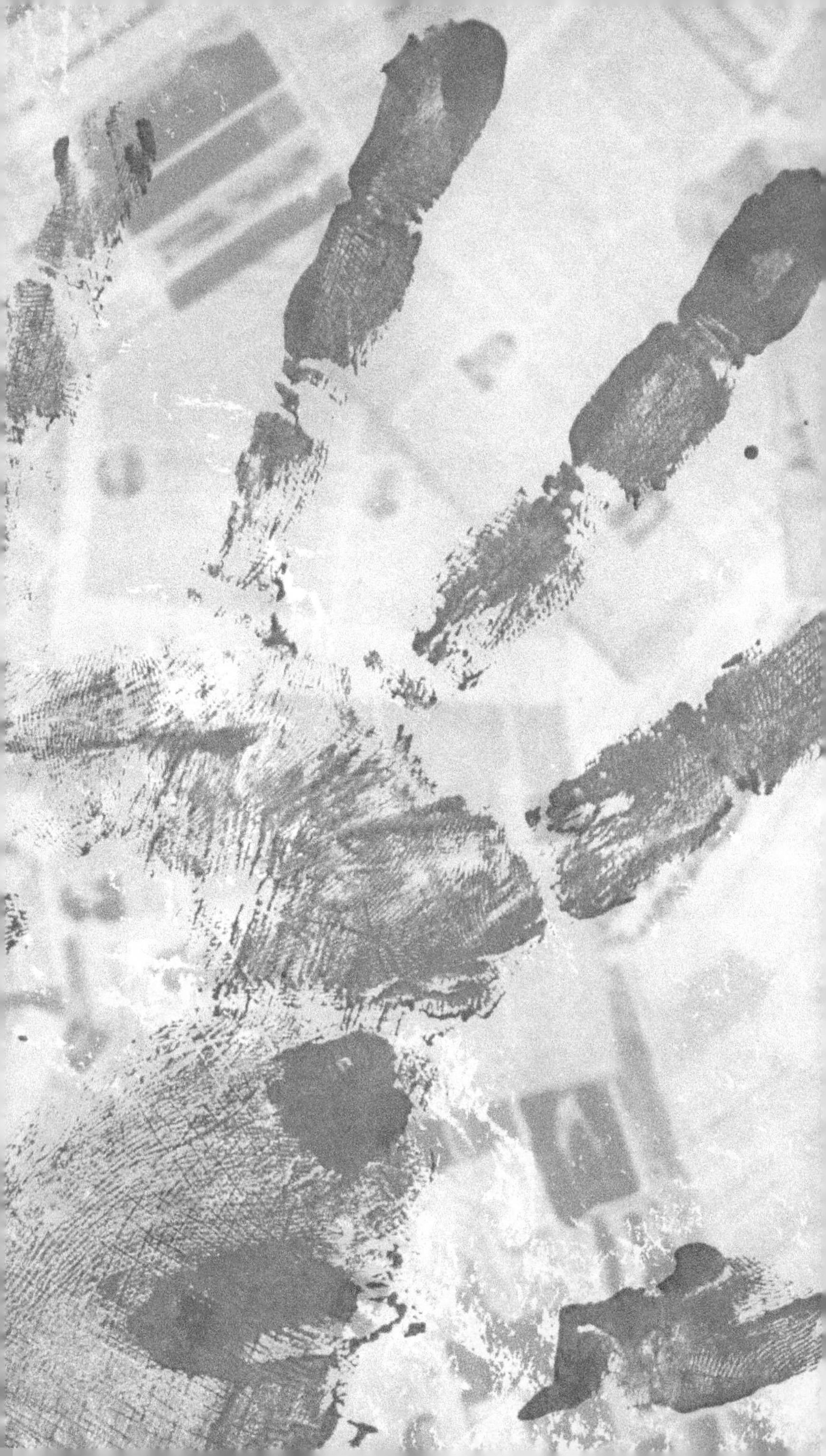

3 YEARS AGO

"WHERE ARE YOU GOING?"

Caine looked over from the couch and smiled softly; I would never tire of that smile.

"Going out for a bit." I tossed my head back, grabbed my bag from the coffee table, and stuffed it with my wallet and keys. "We're out of a few things and I want to make sure we're stocked for the weekend."

I watched as his brows furrowed, calculating. He made us breakfast this morning. He knew we had the essentials, eggs, bread, and milk. Dry pasta was sitting in a box next to a canned sauce for this evening's dinner. I watched as Caine's face morphed from innocent curiosity to hesitant suspicion. We specifically went bulk shopping earlier this month to avoid leaving the house. In his mind, there was no reason I should be abandoning the weekend nest we created.

In any other world, I'd agree.

But we didn't live this fantasy life I once wanted us to live. And so here I was, covering for him. Like I always did.

"Out to see your second husband?"

He started making comments like that lately, and it frustrated me. Even if I knew he was kidding, something about his tone scratched a part of my brain that made me grind my teeth. I almost told him right then and there what it was I was actually doing. But then it would ruin this fun game we had, where we both pretended that we were a perfect little family. My smile was more forced, not as casual as his had been. I think he noticed.

"I'm kidding, Sugar."

"Yeah, yeah, I know." I mumbled. I felt my shoulders shrug subconsciously, and the strap of my tank fell to showcase the skin of my collarbone. His eyes took it as an invitation, wandering over my body.

"Do you have to leave?" he asked wistfully.

"I'll be right back."

My voice was stern enough to make him grumble in his own frustrations, fantasies crushed by a single sentence. At least he wasn't fighting me on it. I blew him a raspberry kiss and slipped out.

I loved these games we played together.

The hardware store was only a ten-minute drive, adjacent to the grocery store. Convenient. The first time I visited, I was young and dumb. The men would corner me in aisles, selling me things I knew I didn't need but wasn't confident to say no to. It was still so new to me then, but now I was a seasoned pro. I came every few weeks, stocking, preparing.

I did it so Caine didn't have to.

I pushed the large cart through the now familiar aisles, looking for my favorite brands of the essentials.

Bleach. Zip Ties. Duct Tape.

Not the same sort of essentials Caine was thinking of, no doubt.

At least he never had to dirty his hands. Not in that way, anyway. Who would suspect me? I stood no taller than five feet, and though I wasn't skinny, I also wasn't strong. As far as anyone else was concerned, I wasn't a threat.

They didn't even blink twice as they rang me up.

Caine watched as I lugged my spoils into the house, the bags weighing me down as I struggled my way over the threshold. This wasn't the secret I was intent on keeping from him. There were only so many things I could keep before I'd explode.

"I didn't think this was what you meant when you said we were out of a few things." His large hands grabbed the bags from my shoulders and I felt immediate relief.

"I needed some stuff for the garden," I argued, "you know, tools and such." He nodded fervently, easily agreeable.

"I will never understand you plant women," his voice rattled as he said it, and his hand moved to the nape of his neck to scratch at it. His tell, or one of them anyway.

"No need to ask, then," I smiled, gesturing to the back door. "To the greenhouse please!"

He did as I asked, and we walked in silence. I wondered if he was thinking the same thing I was.

We were both skirting around the truth, an unspoken agreement.

"I thought you said no garden work this weekend?" Caine dumped the bags onto the floor, opening the tool shed within the greenhouse. I watched as he took out each of my purchases slowly, rolling the tape in his hands and looking at it with a curious light in his eyes before he delicately placed each item in its designated spot.

I shrugged again. He was fishing, but I wouldn't give him what he wanted.

"I can never not be in the garden." I looked around at the greenery around us.

That, at least, wasn't a lie. I found solace here now, secluded in my own world where nothing but my plants mattered.

"Remember when you used to kill everything you touched? What happened to that girl?" Caine tapped my nose with the tip of his finger and we both broke into a burst of comfortable laughter, all uncertainty lost. That's how it would always be between us, I think. It wouldn't take too much to come back to each other again.

"Shut up!" I punched him in the shoulder. "I call it growth."

"You're not wrong, I suppose. I sort of like this Martha Stewart phase you're in. It's...dare I say, adorable?"

My eyes creased and I frowned prominently. It was exaggerated in a way I knew he liked. It made me look innocent. Unassuming.

"Better than you thinking I'm crazy for all of this shit I buy."

"Oh I do," he teased again, "but not for that reason. Think you're crazy, that is." His eyes squinted as he looked at me. It was a look of understanding, of love. It was as close of an admission as I would ever get from him, or a thank you.

We were getting dangerously close to the truth again, and I wondered if it was finally time.

He was my husband, someone I loved and counted on. I would move the world for him, bend to his will at a moment's notice.

And yet, there was something more sinister in his gaze, hidden under that smile. I could feel it, whatever creature lurked beneath his surface, snaking up my spine, wrapping around me and threatening to kill. I knew, in my heart of hearts, that he was dangerous. Even if I hadn't *known*, the challenge in his eyes would be enough to warn me of it. That alone is what kept me from slicing my soul open and spilling every secret I'd kept, for him and from him, onto the floor between us. I wasn't ready to clean up that mess, yet.

My smile didn't reach the corners of my eyes and I think he noticed, but he dropped it. The passion left his face, leaving behind pools of frustration.

"I didn't know I'd married such a gardener." Caine was no longer teasing or pushy. In fact, he sounded rather bored.

"I can finish putting this stuff away, Candy Cane," I said softly, ignoring him. He nodded, hesitating as if he wanted to reach for me before he left me behind. I didn't move until I heard the backdoor shut quietly behind me. A deep sigh escaped me, and I crumpled to the ground.

I didn't know how much longer we could do this to each other.

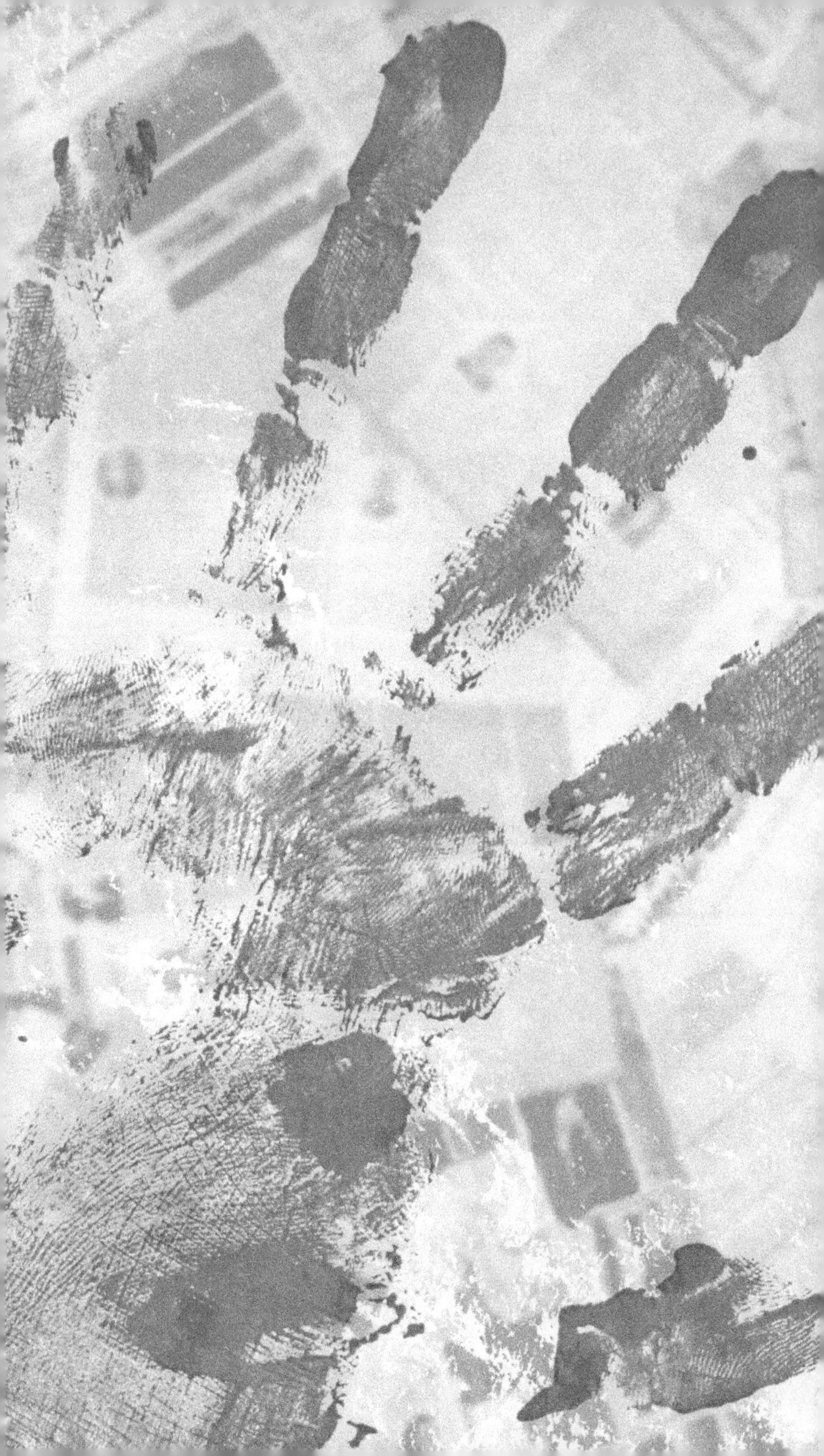

PRESENT DAY

The basement was smaller than I remembered it being, and I felt like it was closing in around me. The walls in my peripherals warped and everything shifted a foot closer. I had to blink once or twice to refocus my eyes, which were flooding with tears each time I remembered the pain several inches below them.

I cut the rest of the lingering rope from my legs, whining as my lips dangled from my face while I hunched over. I almost dropped the knife in my hands from my violent shaking. Weakly, I kicked the rope away, and flew to the stone wall, pressing my hands flush against it, appreciating the coolness for a moment's rest.

I took a deep breath.

"Fuck," I cursed to myself, wishing that I had come down here more than just a handful of times;. I knew almost every nook and cranny of my home, but down here might as well have been another world. I didn't recognize the rooms in the shadows, or the odds and ends Caine left down here. It was a cursed place, a place I refused to return to unless absolutely necessary. That was my fatal flaw.

I wanted to scream. Our neighbors were so close, and if I walked up to the window I'd see their yard. I could hear their dog barking outside, and their calls from the back door to bring him in after he marked their side of the fence. I could call out to them, knowing with full confidence that they would help. I would be free, if only I said something; anything.

As I walked, my hands traced the walls, each finger rubbing along the grooves of the brick. For a second, I wholly and fully *contemplated* screaming. I opened my mouth, waiting to see if sound would come out.

But then, where would that leave me?

I was a good wife, and I had done so well for him, for us. Caine couldn't go to jail. My parents would mourn him, as if it was no better than death. And who would I be? Nothing. Lost, with nothing to show for the achievements I'd gained; the ones no one could ever know. The ones he was, of course, responsible for.

Even as I panicked to free myself from my own personal hell, I didn't want to call to attention the man that put me here. It was convoluted and twisted, but I couldn't stop myself, we were fucked up people. I meant what I said when I told Caine I wouldn't tell anyone. I wouldn't go to the police, or the news. If I were to live tonight—which I surely doubted—I would run away. Hide, do anything in my power to never see him again.

I was afraid I would go back to him if I didn't go far enough.

Which, obviously, wasn't going to happen. Caine would rather cut me open like one of his little projects. It was weird, how your relationship with someone could fall apart in a single day. It didn't matter how close you were, how long you'd been together, or how in sync you thought you were, your connections to people were so delicate. So fragile.

My lips ached and any amount of movement, no matter how subtle, set the fire burning again. I reached to touch them, inspected the damage, and winced against the feeling. I could flick one side, feel it move independently from its partner, and even through the pain I couldn't stop. I couldn't believe he cut me, that he moved his weapon to hurt me. It was so very un-Caine like that I think it shocked the both of us.

I moved my hand away from my mouth, ignoring the blood that came along with it, and listened for his steps. The basement was eerily quiet, and my heart stopped mid beat. Ten seconds passed until I heard his footsteps again. My breathing returned to normal.

I continued in my pursuit—though of what I wasn't sure. I had already done a full circle of the basement, finding little that could help me in my plans to escape. My head lifted, the crease in my brow deepening as I thought. I was smarter than this, I had to be.

The sounds of his steps were closer to the back end of the basement, meaning he was more than likely in our kitchen. Caine always loved to cook. Some of my favorite days were coming home from work to the smells of freshly cooked meatballs and perfectly al dente pasta. I think it was calming for him. It was one of his less chaotic hobbies, anyway. The kitchen, much like the basement, became his safe space, and a place he frequented when he was home.

Our kitchen was in the back of the house, and while there was the back door that would be impossible to get to, the rest of the house was easily feasible. If I can be quiet.

I clutched the knife tightly in my hand and close to my chest. My feet didn't want to move forward, each step was like dragging my leg through layers of mud. But soon enough I was standing in front of the stone stairs, my body shaking. Each step was agony, but I did it. I was grateful Caine didn't finish these steps like I begged him to—concrete was more forgiving than the polished vinyl I'd wanted. I kept my steps soft as I crept up the stairs, but as I approached the door and reached for the handle, I stopped.

I could no longer hear his footsteps, but that wasn't surprising. It was unlikely my ears would pick up on the soft noise from this far away. I had to trust my gut.

I pushed the door open slowly, hating the creaking sound that seemed to echo throughout my house. I knew I was overthinking it; my walls, blessed be, were thick enough that I wouldn't have to worry about a rusty hinge. The slowness of it was agonizing, and my impatience got the better of me. I pushed the door open, my shoulders tensing as it made a loud thud against the wall from the pressure.

Fuck.

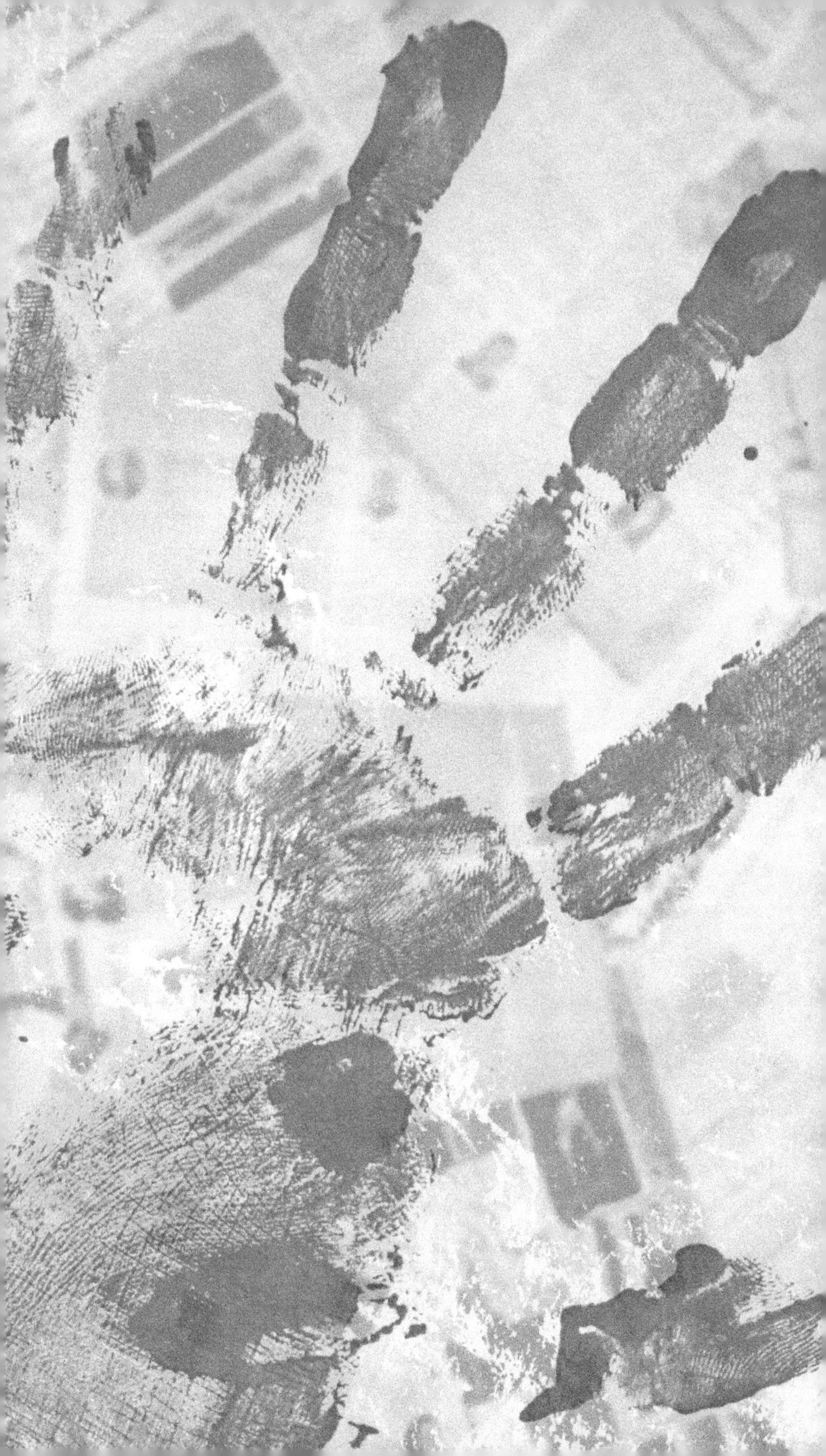

11 YEARS AGO

God, he was just as handsome now as he was when we started dating. There was something about the way he looked at me, with fire and possession; it rooted me to the spot, burned me from the inside. I considered myself a strong woman who held her own, but when it came to Caine, I was weak, and powerless. I could crumble at his feet with only a look.

Our glance lasted no longer than a few seconds, and once his warm, umber eyes dropped from mine, it was like a spell had lifted. I was no longer trapped by him.

I watched as Caine turned to my uncle, laughing at something he said. I wondered sometimes if he thought my family was actually funny. His eyes didn't crinkle the same way they did when he was laughing at *my* jokes. His mouth creased, and his eyes shut as his chest huffed, but his eyes didn't crinkle. Somehow, knowing that he was appeasing my family made me appreciate him even more.

He knew I was still looking at him. I couldn't help it. He dressed exceptionally well today, in khaki shorts that rested at mid-thigh and a collared shirt that he had unbuttoned so far that I could see his chest hair. He never usually dressed this well for my family–he didn't feel the need to prove anything to them because they already loved him, and already considered him a part of the family.

It made me wonder if today was the day.

My father was standing in the corner–like he usually was–but he wasn't glowering, so it was easy to spot that he wasn't in a bad mood. He must not see how obvious it was that Caine was going to propose to me today. I knew daddy didn't love Caine in the same way everyone else did, but he didn't like anyone I dated. I didn't take it personally.

He hasn't said a word yet to Caine, but his eyes trailed us both mercilessly. He wasn't a good man to my mother, but he was always a good father. Protective of me in the ways that mattered. I think he disliked Caine more than the rest of them, but he wasn't vocal enough to tell me to stop dating him.

I don't think I would have listened to him even if he did.

My mother pulled on my arm, pulling me out of my trance.

"Aye, mija, he'll do it lo prometo. Deja de mirar fijamente." Her smile was playful, and I could feel the red creeping up into my cheeks. Where my father's aversion ended, my mother's love flourished. It never surprised me, they always were two sides of one coin. My father was the quiet and observant type, and my mother? She was loud, obnoxious, full of laughter. She loved Caine. She loved Caine for me.

"I'm not staring mama," I tore my arm from her grip, "...just admiring."

"You've been dating for three years. If he doesn't do it tonight he might not have my blessing any longer."

My mother narrowed her eyes and glared daggers into my future husband's back. She was already irritated that Caine hadn't asked them both for permission. Instead, he sat them down, looked at them both with intensity, and told them he would be marrying me. I thought he was going to send my mother into cardiac arrest. Her love ran deep though, and he should be grateful for it.

I could only imagine the face my father made; there was no way it should have ended as well as it did. I shook my head.

He was lucky they already saw him as their adopted son. My mother did, anyway.

"Estará bien, mija." She whispered again.

"I know I know. It's not like I don't know it's coming. I just wish it was here already."

"Dulcie, you know I want nothing more than to throw you the biggest wedding in the history of weddings! I wish it was here already too, but we must be patient." She clapped her hands at the thought.

Caine must have heard—or felt—the sigh that escaped my mouth. We had a way of communicating without any exchanged words, and that was one of my favorite parts about our relationship. It was as if we were one person, not two separate souls. He turned around instinctively, eyebrows raised in concern.

My relationship with my mother was always cordial. We hardly ever fought, she was too much of a timid soul. I envied that about her. I made sure to stay away from topics too serious for her heart to handle, and she responded kindly with warmth and sunshine. Our relationship was not deep, but it was pleasant.

I was not a surface level person. I didn't care so much about big weddings or flowers, I wanted my marriage to be deeper than that. My life with Caine would be shared experiences, good and bad. Not easy—what marriage was?—but that was what made it rewarding.

I rolled my eyes in his direction and he smiled again, though it wasn't long until our internal conversation was interrupted by my cousins and uncles dragging him from the kitchen and through the sliding glass doors to the backyard. I turned back to face my mother, who's eyes lit from the attention.

"I said no big wedding. You know I'm fine hosting it here. It makes more sense that way, I don't want to spend so much money." The light in her eyes dimmed, a furrow creasing in her brow.

"Your father and I work a farm, we make more than enough money—"

"Yes, mama, but Caine and I don't want you both to pay for everything. He feels bad enough that he can't get me a 'proper' wedding ring, whatever that means. He fell victim to that fragile male ego."

"We like him because he's not some spoiled rich boy," she chided, "In no right mind could I abandon my son the way his mama did. We expect nothing from that boy other than for him to love you and cherish you. Which he does. So we're happy to pay for it."

"Lo sé," I smiled. If there was one thing I knew about Caine, it was that I knew he loved me, too.

"How's his job going?" She did this thing where she walked as she started talking, making sure the victim of her conversation would have to follow her. She needed to be close to the boys and, as they ventured further outside, she shadowed their steps. As we walked onto the outdoor porch, my mother closed the sliding door behind us. The boys were now smoking cigars by the pool, and I could tell Caine was uncomfortable. He hated smoking.

"It's okay. He keeps telling me that there's going to be growth coming, but it feels like he's been telling me that for the better half of a year. He keeps working because he really believes it's going to happen. I can't tell him no, not when he gets so passionate about it. You know how he can be."

"Apasionado," she agrees, "I didn't know someone could be so into construction."

"He's up for some sort of lead contractor position, I think. I don't know, he deflects whenever I bring it up. He wants to make sure he can 'provide for his family,' though, so I know he's working hard to get whatever it is. I told him he was full of shit; we'd figure it out without the promotion. But he's like daddy in that way."

I knew it was the wrong thing to say when my mother's shoulders tensed. We tried not to talk about the horrors and pain my father could inflict, verbally and physically. Mama would never leave him, and despite it all, I couldn't believe he was a bad person. His actions sort of just... got swept under the rug. It was hard to hate my dad when it wasn't me he was so awful to.

I shimmied uncomfortably, settling in one of her rocking chairs. She followed suit.

"I'm sure he will be a great husband, Dulcie. You deserve everything this whole wide world can give you."

My mother gazed outward, past the men that stood before us with puffs of smoke coming out of their lungs. Instead, her eyes rested on the horizon, just past the cotton fields on their property. I could tell that she was leaving me now, lost in her own world. It was better that way, disassociating from the pain she'd endured these years. At least the bruises were less noticeable now.

I took the time to single Caine out again. He would be a good husband, I was as certain of that as I could be about anything. I wouldn't have to worry about him hurting me.

"There you are, Sugar!" he yelled towards me, waving his hands exuberantly. As if he hadn't just seen me. The boys laughed at him, and I could see them rolling their eyes at us. I loved that about him, that he was so unapologetically on 'Team Dulcie' all the time. Caine was never embarrassed to be around me. Or my family. I smiled and waved back.

Caine took that as an invitation, and he walked towards me with purpose, ignoring the catcalls from my family.

My mother turned to look at him with envy in her eyes as he grabbed me from the chair and enveloped me in a hug. He was looking for a reason to escape the smoke, and looking for a reason to touch me. Caine overshadowed me, crushing me to his chest with his huge, calloused hands. I laughed as his breath tickled my neck, and firm, possessive kisses touched the spot behind my ear. It was such a public display of claim, no better than if he had marked his territory like a dog.

"Sweet Sugar, I missed you." He whispered in my ear.

"We've been in the same place for four hours." I shook my head against his chest. Caine let go long enough to look at my mother, then me. He shrugged his shoulders.

"Oy, tortolitos!" One of my uncles called our way. Mother rolled her eyes again and shushed him from her seat.

Caine smiled, the familiar wrinkles lining his face. God, he was so handsome.

I could be on 'Team Caine' forever.

PRESENT DAY

My mistake could mean the end of my life.

My heart raced so fast I could feel it beating outside of my chest. I snapped my head back and forth, looking for a place to hide. I know I said I knew my house like the back of my hand—and I did—but everything was five times harder when I was panicking. It felt like every good decision, and everything I knew about myself and the place I lived disappeared from my mind. There was nothing in my head, no matter how hard I tried to grasp at strings of memory.

I only had a few seconds to spare. Caine would not have heard the creaking of a door, but he surely heard the thud. I tried to take a breath and place myself.

I was standing in my hallway. To the right and left of me were our respective offices, and in front of me the living room. I wasn't the type of woman that loved an open concept like most my age and, in this moment, I was thankful for it. Caine would have to walk through the dining room, the family room and then the living room and their various furnishings and doorways before he would be able to see me. It wouldn't exactly be an obstacle course, but it would help my cause.

He was probably getting close, but I was still thankful for the walls and close corners I had in my favor. I grabbed for the door—the fucking traitor— and shut it behind me quietly, pressing myself flat against the wall as I tiptoed into the office to my right. Caine's office, actually.

I shut this door too, placing my hands flat on the wood as I took in deep quiet breaths. I had just a moment to spare.

He was almost impossible to miss. His confident steps were loud—the sounds of a man walking around comfortably in his home. No one outside would know the wiser; I'm sure our home looked pleasantly normal as an onlooker. Night must have settled by now, and unless he had turned on the lights on his way, we would look like nothing but another suburban home.

I listened as Caine opened the door to the basement to whistle at me.

"Are you making noise down there, Sugar? Do I need to come help you?" There was a rustling sound in his hand, like he had grabbed our first aid kit from underneath the kitchen sink. Like band aids were going to fix the mess of my lip. I grimaced, remembering the pain I had gratefully started to ignore. I wavered as I stood, the loss of blood affecting my balance.

Without an answer, Caine's concerned voice deepened in frustration.

"It's rude to ignore someone, Dulcie. You know that!"

My hands were starting to shake again, and I moved them quickly to avoid rattling the door.

This person with the rough voice and the sharp knives—that wasn't my husband. That wasn't the Caine I knew.

Even when I knew what he was doing down there, I don't think I had ever been afraid of him. Even when Caine hurt other people, he could never hurt me.

Now, as I listened with nothing but a thin piece of wood between us, I was petrified.

"Dulcie, Sugar, I'm only going to ask one more time."

His voice sharpened, malice tinting each word. I stayed deathly still.

"I'm coming down there!" His threats turned into a yowl, and I heard as he descended the stairs again. I wasted no time before I opened the bedroom door and rushed to shut him down in the basement, trapping him.

Fuck being quiet.

I heard his frustrated growl down in the darkness, and a small huff escaped me as I shoved my shoulder into the basement door, hoping my meager frame would be enough to hold him. Caine had the mind to padlock it, and I sent a prayer to the gods that I could wrap my fingers around it and lock it. It clicked into place comfortably. Only then did I release the pressure of my body weight from the door, panting from effort.

Feeling safer, I turned around and whipped my head in both directions, forgetting where I last saw my phone. I needed to get help. It might have been too late, but someone needed to know what he had done.

And what he was doing to me.

A loud knock from behind me startled me, my breath catching in the back of my throat.

"Dulcie!" He screamed, pounding on the door and rattling the doorknob. The padlock stayed in place, keeping him locked down in his own hellhole. My breathing evened slightly at the reassurance. "Let me out of here! You fucking bitch!"

I kicked the door with my foot, sending a shooting pain through my leg and into my hips.

"Fucking piece of shit," I seethed, "I can't wait to see your face behind bars."

He had no other response but more screaming and pounding, and I stepped away from the basement and into the living room.

My bag wasn't on the couch, or on the coffee table.

Where did I put it?

I spent the next few minutes scrambling, digging through the cushions and rushing back and forth between rooms. It wasn't the best use of my time, I should have used my freedom to escape for good, but what had I said about losing all common sense while in an active threat? I made note—if I made it out alive—to never discredit those in horror movies ever again.

No one knew what it was like until you were put in that same situation.

I finally found it in the kitchen, torn from its charger that was plugged into the wall. My hands left traces of blood on the screen as I punched in the familiar passcode. There was hardly any service; my kitchen only ever had one bar, max. Our home backed up against a mess of overgrown brush and forest, two acres separating me from the freeway.

We were at the end of a road, Caine's idea, as he wanted the privacy.

In hindsight, it was a terrible idea. Another regret I would have to add to the list, if I survived.

All of that to say, the kitchen was the farthest away from our closest cell tower. The freeway could have been a good option, but no one would stop for me. Not at this time of night, and not as I dripped in sweat and blood. I looked like I was an unhinged criminal.

I stood there for so long that I hadn't noticed that Caine's pounding and screams stopped. There was nothing but the sound of my own breathing and my thoughts screaming at me to move. I looked at my phone again, eyebrows furrowing when I noticed it sitting at a measly two percent.

Seconds were beginning to feel like hours. It was like I was drowning in quicksand, each movement of my fingers moving impossibly slow as they glided over each number, while the world around me blurred.

I didn't realize I had started to cry, tears now staining my cheeks as they cascaded down and coated the screen. The numbers were so large that they taunted me, ridiculed me, and forced me to swallow deja vu. I had the opportunity to end this all those years ago, and I failed.

This time, 911 was failing *me.*

2 YEARS AGO

I THINK IF SOMEONE WERE TO ASK ME, I'D TELL THEM that my favorite season was summer. Not the kind of summer with pools, sunshine, or layers of thick, creamy sunscreen. My favorite type of summer was right now, at the end of August, when the bugs were at their worst and the heat was a slow burn instead of a passionate affair. It was when I could feel the wetness drifting through the air, sticking to my body and my clothes. Like a sauna without having to sit in a dark room at the gym.

I slapped a mosquito that was stealing the blood from my arm, smearing it across the hair on my skin and flicking its carcass to the ground. I was starting to get used to the blood. I remembered having passed out from the sight of it a few times in my youth, but that aversion was almost all gone by now.

I was sweating, and the greenhouse was hotter than hell. But I fucking loved it.

Feeling satisfied, I wiped the sweat from my brow and sent a quick prayer for my now-dead mosquito friend. I used to avoid killing insects, but the last few years have hardened me. Death was a part of life. A cruel, sometimes unnecessary part of life, but a bridge we all one day would cross.

For some, that day was sooner than it was for others.

I cooed at the parsley plant next to me, thanking it as I cut a few stray stems from its body. Not death for this sweet boy, but maiming for the benefit of others. It felt like an omen, somehow, though I didn't really believe in those anymore.

Caine knew my day would be spent in the greenhouse by the garden, as they so often were anymore, and he requested freshly cut herbs to cook with later this evening. By the position of the sun, I reckoned he wasn't too far behind. An hour, maybe.

I got up from my knees and delicately curled my fingers over the stems, leaving the greenhouse and my injured parsley plant behind. I abandoned the rest of my tiny, living projects, clicking the door into place and patting it with satisfaction before I stepped away. The greenhouse was situated perfectly, backed up against the forest of trees and only twenty feet from our home. I smiled as I neared the house, turning around to catch one last glimpse of it—my safe haven.

I never thought that I'd be good at gardening. I wasn't exactly a green thumb, and it took so much effort to keep things from dying under my care. Sometimes I still walked in to find I'd overwatered something, or neglected another for too long. It kept me moving, and made me direct my attention to something other than the horror I lived through day to day. Taking care of the greenhouse was good for me.

When I originally proposed the idea, I thought Caine would have laughed in my face. He didn't, though. I thought it was because he believed in me. Now, the more I contemplate it—why did I ever let myself be alone to think

—the more I realized he was just looking for something else to take my time and attention.

It was his downfall that my only hobby would ever truly be him.

It was my downfall too.

I sighed deeply, crushing the parsley with my fingers as a strange spasm caused my hand to squeeze tighter. Thinking was dangerous. Thinking was bad.

After rinsing the herbs in the sink and leaving them for later, I stood comfortably in the heat of the kitchen, moving to quiet music in my head. With all of the windows open the sun did its job, toasting me in that way I loved so much this time of the year. I did turn on the air conditioning eventually—Caine would be pissed if he came home the way it was. At one point this week he complained that the feeling was like stepping into an oven. I rolled my eyes at his exaggeration, but the house would be a crisp sixty-nine degrees by the time he got home from work. Too cold for my liking, but for Caine it was worth it. A little discomfort for me was nothing to complain about.

It could be much worse, I reminded myself, as I had so often lately.

I continued to move. Like the garden, dancing was a way to let out all of my anxious energy. I never actually turned on music, instead letting the songs that infiltrated my head push each limb and every muscle into motion.

Anyone looking into my windows would be caught off guard by my erratic motions. I never said I was a good dancer. I'd say I looked particularly insane, actually. My laugh echoed through the halls and I kicked off my shoes, laughing harder at the loud thud as they hit the wall in the corner. The muscles in my core screamed in pleasure as I doubled over, the soft pads of my feet tapping against the floor.

Thirty minutes until the love of my life returned to me. I really needed to get myself together. I needed to get a job, another hobby, anything else but this. I feared I was losing myself, falling prey to the hidden demons that lay dormant inside of me. They wanted to come out and play.

God damn it, Caine. Why did you do this to me?

I tried to slow my body and take more intentional steps. My calculated movements were not enough when I didn't watch where I was going; my legs were still moving faster than my brain could keep up. I stepped and slipped on something silky smooth and soft, and my heart lurched as I felt myself falling to my hands and knees.

The laughter died in my throat.

Tangled in my bare toes were tendrils of hair. Immediately my hand went to my head, searching the long strands as if I would find the source of the intruder there. But the color didn't look right.

It was thin and blonde, the opposite of my dark brunette roots. Caine's cropped hair wasn't near long enough to be the origin either. It was a stranger to me, to my home.

But not to Caine.

I closed my eyes and rocked back onto my butt, pulling the hair from my toes and throwing it. It didn't go far, floating through the air until it delicately settled back on the ground. *My* ground. Her hair was on *my* ground, in *my* home.

I screamed. The sound was much too big for my body, and it was so strong that it completely took the wind from my ribcage. It was so loud that it rattled the walls around me. It was so big that I could have sworn that I lost a bit of myself after it. Spit scattered onto the floor, pieces of me that I would no longer get back. A version of who I was died in that scream.

My hands scrambled to push myself away, not realizing I was now backed against the basement door. It was everywhere all at once, the horror. I couldn't escape it, and I knew I was too deep. It was going to consume me.

Twenty minutes.

My breathing was ragged, but I had to calm myself down. I couldn't lose myself, not now. Being out in the garden all day, it made sense how I could have missed this, but I wished to God that I didn't. My lifetime of cleaning up after him never prepared me for this. His lack of self preservation. No attention to detail. His *fucking* arrogance.

There was no rulebook for this.

I opened my eyes.

Still sitting against the wall, I pushed my back against it to get into a comfortable squat. I reached for the hair once more. It shouldn't scare me, it was just hair, after all. The source was somewhere in the dump, among millions of other pieces of discarded trash. She wouldn't come after me. I stroked the strand in my hand, such a different texture than the parsley I practically crushed only moments before. It already seemed like a lifetime ago.

I stood up, thoughts of dancing and forgetting gone. I tried hard to refocus, to find the wife that saved her husband. She was hidden here somewhere in this body of mine. I stood up, still clutching the abandoned tendrils of dead blonde hair.

Of dead blonde.

Of blonde.

Of *dead.*

I fisted my free hand. I had to breathe. I only had fifteen

minutes until he'd be home, and that was if I was as well tuned to Caine's schedule as I thought I was.

Quickly I walked around my home, passing through like a ghost. The music in my head was gone, replaced by fast moving thoughts. I burst through the back door again, looking not to my greenhouse, but to a small hole in the ground thirty feet to the right of it.

"Firewood. I need firewood." I chanted to myself. I feared the slower I moved, the easier my brain would forget. Focus was not coming easily, not when the demons danced behind my eyes.

It was easily locatable, thankfully, stacked neat and pretty by the edge of the porch. I shoved his transgressions into my front pocket, shaking my fingers to disentangle the leftovers. I'd only seen Caine do this on his own, and only once or twice. The heat was simmering down into a warm summer evening, and the sun was dropping by the second. Everything felt so rushed I was afraid I couldn't keep up with it.

Ten minutes.

The fire starter was hidden but I found it eventually, my hands were cut from moving the wood and other tools in the storage container he kept close to the house. I took the wood and the fire starter to the hole opposite my greenhouse, dumping them to the ground as I looked deep into the fire pit.

He dug this out right after we got married, convinced we would use it every weekend for the rest of our lives. I could count on one hand the amount of times in the last nine years we actually did.

My feet pushed the wood into the pit several feet down. I got down on all fours, placing the fire starter right in the middle. It almost took the entire length of my arm, and my breathing quickened as I hoisted myself back up.

The panic returned. Fuck, I needed a lighter.

Five minutes.

The sun completely disappeared, and the only available light source available to me now was the lights I left on in the house. I returned to the tool box using my makeshift lighthouse, digging around until I wrapped my hands around the lighter. The pit was taunting me, seeming to grow in size as I approached it again. I fell flat on my stomach, reaching the lighter to the center where the fire starter proudly sat.

The flames started small, flickering so softly I wondered if I had done it wrong. Until it didn't. The fire engulfed the pit in its entirety after a few moments, consuming every piece of splintered wood until it stood three feet tall. I smiled, pleased with myself.

I only had a few seconds to spare, completely forgetting why I'd gone to all the trouble. My shaking fingers found the pocket of my jeans, pulling out the blonde hair I'd found.

I threw it into the fire, watching as it curled and darkened, burnt until it was evidence no more. It was gone like the girl I had no name for, smoke rising from the pit and disintegrating into the already warm night air.

"What the fuck are you doing, Dulcie?"

My head snapped around, a humorous look of both confusion and apprehension from my heart standing in the doorway.

"I did it myself!" I said lightly, feeling so much more at ease, as I did while I was dancing. It was over, it was gone and I could be myself again. The wife that loved her husband, not the one that feared him.

"You...started a fire? In the middle of summer?"

He didn't get it.

"Sugar, it's hotter than hell outside. Put that out and let's go inside." He frowned, holding the back door open and beckoning me forward. "Did you pick those herbs for me? I'll make us pasta."

I ground my teeth and ran my tongue across the back of my gums. He *really* didn't get it, what this meant to me. I was getting emotional over a damn bonfire, but his lack of appreciation made my mouth go dry. He was reaping the benefits, yet I received no rewards for the crimes I committed for him.

"Yeah, in the sink. I just washed them."

Caine saw the difference in my tone, though I tried my best to hide my resentment. His eyebrows creased, his lip turned up in a bit of a snarl.

His glamor flickered more than usual lately. Gone was the pleasing man that kept up appearances, and in its place was someone detached and indifferent. In fact, sometimes it felt like a challenge, like he wanted me to see. Like he was begging me to invite myself into his hellhole.

"What's your problem?" he grunted. I crossed my arms in front of me. Not even a proper acknowledgement for the fucking parsley.

"I did *this*," I gestured to the fire behind me, "all by myself. I did this for *us*. I just want to be appreciated for the work I put in." There was a double meaning behind those words, and I felt my pent up frustrations ready to spill from my mouth like sickness.

His hand ran through his head, and Caine's exasperated look made me dig my heels further into the soft soil. We both were not ones to give in, easily.

"I've had a long day, Dulc. The last thing I want to do is

clean up your mess. I just want to eat and go to bed." I felt my jaw slack.

"Are you kidding me?" He started to retreat into the house, but I followed him aggressively. "Clean up *my* mess? I don't think that's the argument you want to ma-"

"Dulcie!" Caine spun around, stopping me dead in my tracks. The words died in my throat as we stared at each other. His fingers twitched, and I imagined him wrapping his hands around my neck; as I watched his eyes find my jugular, I was sure he was thinking the same thing.

"Put it out, please. I really, really don't want to fight with you right now." Caine was still loud, but he softened his delivery. It was that save that stopped me from spitting ugly words back at him. Heat burned from my cheeks. I couldn't respond, and didn't want to give him the satisfaction of winning. I knew I was the person he needed most, I was irreplaceable. That win was enough for me, for now.

I stormed past him instead, my shoulder brushing his chest as I slipped by and retreated to the safety of our bathroom. I shut the door loudly, praying he wouldn't follow.

He didn't, and wouldn't.

Instead I heard him outside, chucking wood around and smothering the flame that I'd been so proud of. He beat that fire into submission as he had done to me over the years. I closed my eyes as I imagined its light dimming, its patience wearing thin as it gave up its fight.

That fire was so much like me.

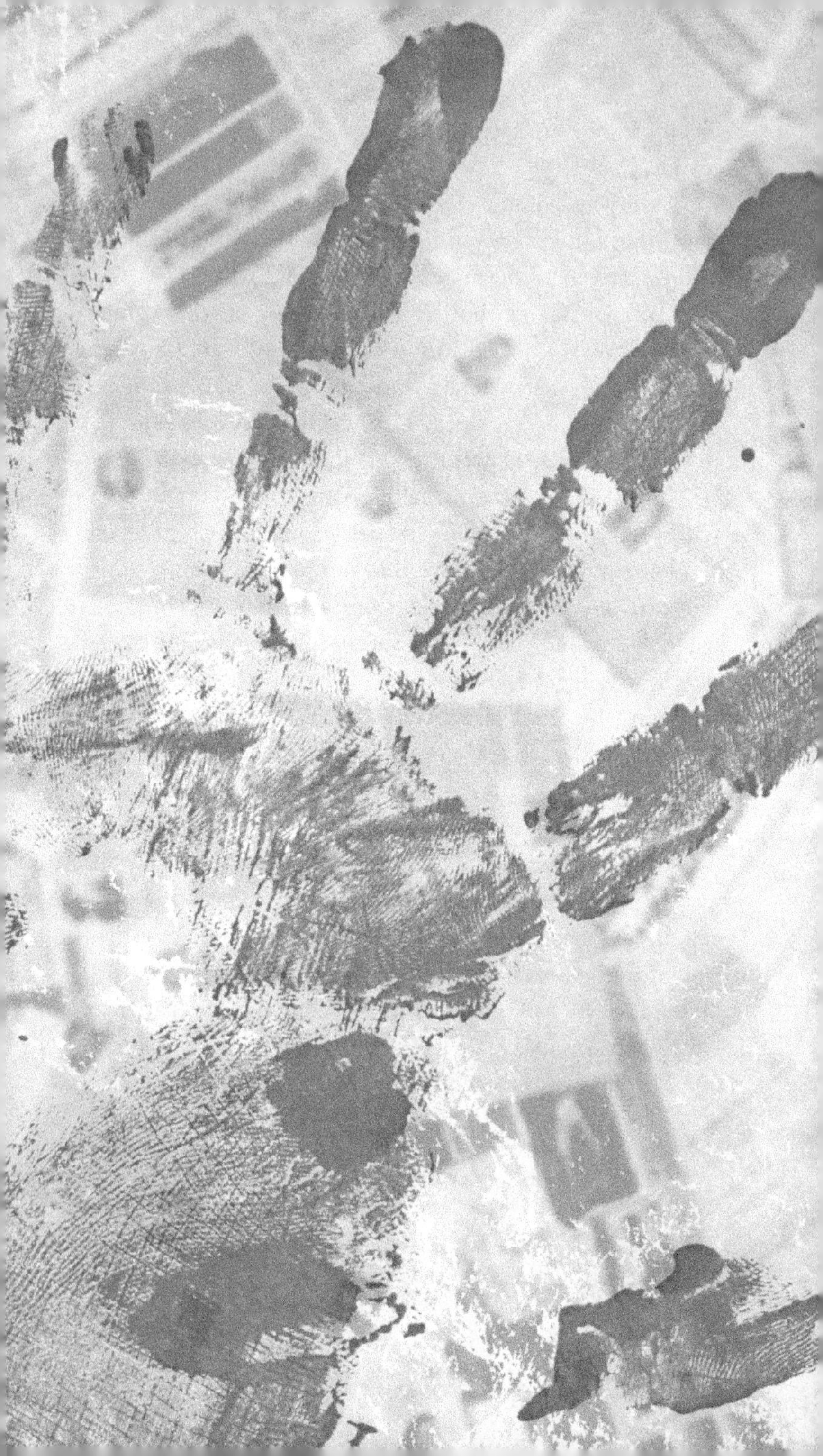

PRESENT DAY

Caine's pounding returned, but it sounded different than its previous fist driven thuds. This sound was harder, faster, more dangerous. I had forgotten that I left him down in his own lair, a place where he had more tools than I could fathom that could tear a person limb from limb. I needed to go, now.

Tossing my phone against the countertop again, the useless piece of shit, I tried to run. That's when I heard the crack. The basement door shattered; even being just a few rooms down I could hear pieces of it colliding against the walls and crumble to the floor.

Another slam from something heavy—though I wasn't sure what—and the door finally gave way.

Accompanying the splintered wood shards was a thunderous crunch as his thick boots stepped through the mess he was creating. I could hear Caine whack away at the door with his weapon of choice, and my heart dropped into the pit of my stomach.

"You thought you could keep me away," he cooed, out of breath and panting. Caine was not a small guy by any stretch of the word, he worked out regularly, and his athletic passions kept him in shape. I didn't want to know what it was he was carrying that made him breathe the way he was.

If my heart could drop any lower, it would.

I stood frozen in fear, like a deer caught in the headlights. When his thrashing started quieting into small, barely indistinguishable sounds, I snapped out of my haze and turned around. I ducked below the island situated in the center of the kitchen, trying to pull at the knobs to find a place to hide. I couldn't remember why on Earth I opted for these fake cabinets.

Aesthetic? God fucking damn it.

"Dulcie c'mon, I just want to talk to you!" Caine's voice had that dangerous edge to it again, and my stomach churned as I heard him walk through our living room. His feet were slow, but steady, and he traced my steps from the basement to where I now hid in the kitchen, my arms hugging my knees.

"I know you're here, baby. You couldn't leave me."

I hated how right he was, how I couldn't sprint out of the front door the minute I shut him down there. How I didn't leave him after I watched the terrible shit he did. I could have been halfway across town by now, and instead I signed my own death certificate.

"It didn't have to be this way. It could have been so easy if you just..."

He didn't finish his sentence, it seemed to catch in the back of his throat.

Instead, his heavy boots echoed in the silence. I pressed my hand firmly against my mouth. Pain erupted so harshly that my eyes practically rolled to the back of my head; it took every ounce of resolve to not cry out in agony. With my lips barely hanging on, just the lightest touch sent them into a ferocious throbbing rhythm. My breaths were hot against my palm, and I felt a tear crawl down my cheek, soaking my fingertips. When I pulled my hand away, it wasn't just tears that glistened across each pad, but blood that came with it.

I forgot just how delicate and fragile I was. As my adrenaline waned, so did my motivation to survive. My head was dizzy, and I was going to faint from the wounds inflicted upon me, and the accompanying blood loss.

I should have moved, but I couldn't. Even with all the willpower in the world, my feet wouldn't move an inch. I shifted my weight onto my toes and leaned forward, forcing myself to try. Caine dropped something heavy on the floor, and I could feel the vibrations through the soles of my feet. I could hear the blade of whatever it was he was holding being dragged across our floor. I wanted to scream at him for ruining the perfect image we'd pulled off for so long, and for what we had become in just a night.

"Sugar, I wished I could have just looked away. I didn't want to see you. But I did. You didn't move fast enough. This really is your fault, you know."

I wrapped around the island, hoping I was fast enough to avoid him. His voice felt like it was everywhere all at once, and I wasn't sure where I was even running to, anymore.

"You didn't even look afraid of me. Which I guess, is a good thing. I didn't want to have to fight you more than I had to." I felt the strands on my hair tug behind me. My eyes closed tight, my tears now free flowing. Caine grabbed my hair and pulled harder, snapping my neck back. The bones cracked and I whined in pain. When I opened my eyes I could see him smiling down at me.

"Boo," he whispered, before slamming my head against the hard wood of the island.

I saw stars.

He didn't stop, every swing of his arm sent my face crashing into the cabinets until my head ached from exhaustion and horror. I felt my body go limp as yet another crash of pain washed over me.

I started flailing, and to Caine's surprise I grabbed a hold of the weapon in his hand—a long axe shaped...thing —and pulled it from his grip. The weight of the tool surprised me and it crashed to the ground with a heavy thud. It did what it was intended to, however, and Caine cursed under his breath as he loosened the reins on my head. I pulled my face forward and away from his grip, wincing as more than several strands of hair were left behind in his hand.

"Bitch!" He screamed again.

I grabbed the axe from the ground and swung. It didn't really matter where it landed. My aim wasn't great, but the wooden handle caught on his shin behind me. I heard Caine's scream, and I did it again. If only I had gotten him with the blade.

Annoyed, Caine reached for me again. I dodged his grip and crawled on all fours around the island until I stumbled onto my feet. He moved quickly, stomping close behind me, just a fingertip away from having me in his grasp.

"Stay the fuck away from me," I warned him, stabilizing myself on my feet as I stared into his black eyes. The axe hung loosely in my grip, swinging gently back and forth.

I could have sworn I saw flames reflected in his irises. I never knew this man to be this angry; it was starting to make me angry, too.

"Were you ever honest with me?" I hissed. Silence. "Ten years. Did you do this for ten years? Did I ever know the real you, or did we live in a fucking lie?"

There was a flicker of something, but I was too charged to notice it.

"You have the devil inside of you, Caine." I spit the words at him like daggers, begging them to bury themselves in his chest. "The fucking devil. I don't know you."

"You're mistaken, Dulcie." I stepped backward at the warning in his voice. "You know me. You know me more than anyone."

I backed up so far that I ran into the countertop. The sudden pressure felt like the walls were closing in on me again. I felt my heart race, and the axe shook in my grip.

"What were you doing that day, Dulcie?"

"I don't know what you mean."

Caine's fist tightened into a close grip, and I watched as he slammed it down on the island so hard it should have hurt. He gave no impression that it did.

"I'm sick of playing games!" He yelled. "You're not stupid and I won't be tricked into thinking that you are. You shouldn't have been there. You told me you weren't going to go downstairs. You never go downstairs."

I wanted to tell him. He was so close to the truth—it almost felt like he was digging for it. It was like he knew. He had already admitted it, right?

We fucking knew each other, just like he said.

Instead, my teeth clamped shut. I wouldn't give him the satisfaction.

"I came down to end it for good," I said, lying through my thin lips.

"Liar."

"I came to end it. To leave you. I was done with this shit, Caine."

It hurt me to throw those words at him. I didn't mean it, I couldn't mean it. He slammed his fists on the island again.

"Take it back." I could barely hear him through his closed lips.

"Ten years down the drain, Caine. And it's all because of you."

I screamed as he launched himself at me.

1 YEAR AGO

I WAS TIRED.

So fucking tired.

Everything around me was still and quiet, and even the crickets stopped chirping this late in the evening. My bed enveloped me, with plush pillows and a large queen-size comforter wrapping around me so tight that I could feel myself slipping deeper and deeper into our mattress. Into nothing.

And yet, I couldn't sleep. The space beside me felt as large and as cavernous as the Sahara Desert. Empty and lonely, I cocooned myself until I was afraid I'd disappear. God, I hated sleeping alone. I wanted to be married because it meant that I wouldn't have to anymore. I would always have someone to touch my cold feet to underneath the covers, and someone to press flush against my back as a tether to reality while I was lost in dreams.

I didn't know, at the time, that my life would turn out the way it did. Even married, I didn't have any of that. Those hopes and wishes were lost several years in.

I was going to sleep alone for the rest of my life.

It was well past midnight by now, and my eyes, though hurting from the strain of blinking, would not stay shut. I tried shutting down, leaving consciousness for nightmares, but my body failed me. It would not give me just this one victory.

I quit counting the minutes until Caine returned, almost as frightened of his arrival as I was of him never returning at all. My hands grasped the inside of my comforter instead, squeezing with each breath I took. The silence was so strong it was deafening, and I cursed the silent crickets and Caine's ongoing absence.

Another hour must have passed before I heard the creaking of our front door. He never did fix it as he promised; it was one of those things that grew in the pit of my stomach, the seed of resentment blossoming into something larger and more prominent with each recognition. When it opened fully, the door collided with the back end of the wall, shattering the illusion of stillness. It was as if he'd forgotten my presence entirely, or didn't care at all.

It was quiet for a moment longer, and I cocked my head in the direction of the doorway in case I missed it.

I knew he wasn't coming to bed, not yet anyway.

A loud thump made me jump, causing me to burrow deeper into my fortress of blankets.

And then there were footsteps.

"Dulcie, sugar, are you awake?" His voice was hoarse, a product of adrenaline and overstimulation. I knew my husband. It was the same voice I got when he was excited, low and sultry. Dangerously predatory.

I refused to answer. Despite my loneliness, I was petrified of this version of him. It was one I'd seen so many times before, right before he got the urge. I squeezed my eyes shut, exaggerating each inhale and exhale; hoping he would leave me be. Tonight was not going to be the night he'd find out my secret, I wasn't sure I'd survive it.

Caine seemed satisfied, backing up slowly and quietly shutting the door as he retreated. His steps had more pep to them after he left me, and he galloped across the floors as if he'd dodged the bullet of a lifetime. I felt a tear travel down my cheek as more unusual noises followed. I didn't want to know them, didn't want to hear them. I wished I was dead, far away from this place where my husband killed women and stole my innocence from me.

I was always here when he brought them home. It was my least favorite part about it all, knowing those people got to see him that way. They would never be able to see the Caine I loved, the one so many of us cared for. They would only see the evil in him, the horror.

The screaming started at around one thirty.

They were ugly screams. I could picture her as clearly in my mind as if he'd showcased her right in front of me. She had red hair that looked like it could catch fire at any moment. Her cheeks were round and freckled. She was so different from me.

By the sound of the thuds as he dragged her through our home and into his dungeon of toys, she was not small. I think that was the only similarity between us. I imagined thick thighs and a gloriously curved hip that layered over her tight jeans. She was beautiful even in my thoughts. And now she was gone.

Did Caine appreciate her as much as I did?

Caine was quiet after that, cleaning up his work, reeling in satisfaction and cockiness. I could see the smug look on his face, and the sweat that inevitably formed at the creases of his eyes.

The girl he'd brought home was no more. I didn't get to

see her or meet her, and honestly I don't know if I would have even wanted to. My gut reeled in guilt. Even if I didn't do it, I did it. I allowed it to happen, in my house, underneath my nose. I could have stopped it.

But I wouldn't.

The house was mute again. A deathly still silence, the kind that freaked me out. It was the in-between pieces, the gaps where his urge was done and the after would begin. It wasn't peaceful like you would think, and my eyes—though heavy—were not going to close anytime soon.

I listened for the dragging noise as he came back upstairs. I knew his routine by now, I knew trash bags full of her would make skid marks on my floor. I knew he would be wiping it with bleach and a towel. I knew him, and in some twisted way, I knew her too. I knew what had become of her.

The shower started. I think that was the worst part about it. Not the killing, not the maiming. It was this part, how he showered and cleaned himself up. How he spent time washing the evidence of her existence from him, like she didn't matter at all.

When he crawled into bed with me, I was visibly shaking. He wrapped blankets around me tightly, knowing I would complain about the cold in the morning. He was a great husband, at the end of it all. He pressed up against me, our backs touching. He smelled like fresh musk, like pine trees and body wash.

At least I wasn't alone.

He was gone by the time I woke up. I stretched my legs and arched my back, hating how large the bed was and how small I felt inside of it. My hands ached and cramped, and I stretched them, cracking each knuckle to avoid the soreness.

When I was up and walking around—making sure my feet were covered in socks with grips—I searched our home. I didn't want to find anything, I prayed he'd cleaned up every bit of his urge last night. My patience was easing, chipping away like leaves falling from their trees in the dead of fall.

I tapped my feet against the wood, relieved that I didn't come across what looked like a crime scene. I only had one thing to check off my To-Do list today. It came to me in the middle of the night when I was in a deep REM sleep, and now it was the only thing I could think about.

The screams I heard last night, they weren't just for me. They were for everyone. With walls so thin, anyone could hear them.

Stupid Caine. Silly Caine. So irresponsible, unable to cover himself. He'd be in jail if not for me.

I needed to soundproof the basement.

I couldn't go down there, he would know, especially so soon after he got rid of her body. I also had no desire to enter that cursed space. I needed to get to the windows. The air was crisp and cool as I exited my home, touching open skin and sliding under my thin clothes. I shivered, but I couldn't tell if it was from the bone chilling cold or my body's way of letting the anxiety leak through.

The window wells on the sides of the house were normal looking, exactly what I expected. Large metal structures surrounded it, covered by thin plastic to prevent rainwater. Nothing to alarm anyone of his misgivings, not unless they heard him.

I pulled out my phone and opened up a hidden search engine. My fingers flew past the keyboard, there was no way they could tie this to him. The rains would come here, they always did. We were homeowners that backed a forest. It was the responsible thing to do, to protect your home from flooding. It happened to everyone. We were just overly cautious.

No one will know.

I stared down at the text in the search field, the results staring up at me. Blinding me.

How to install storm windows.

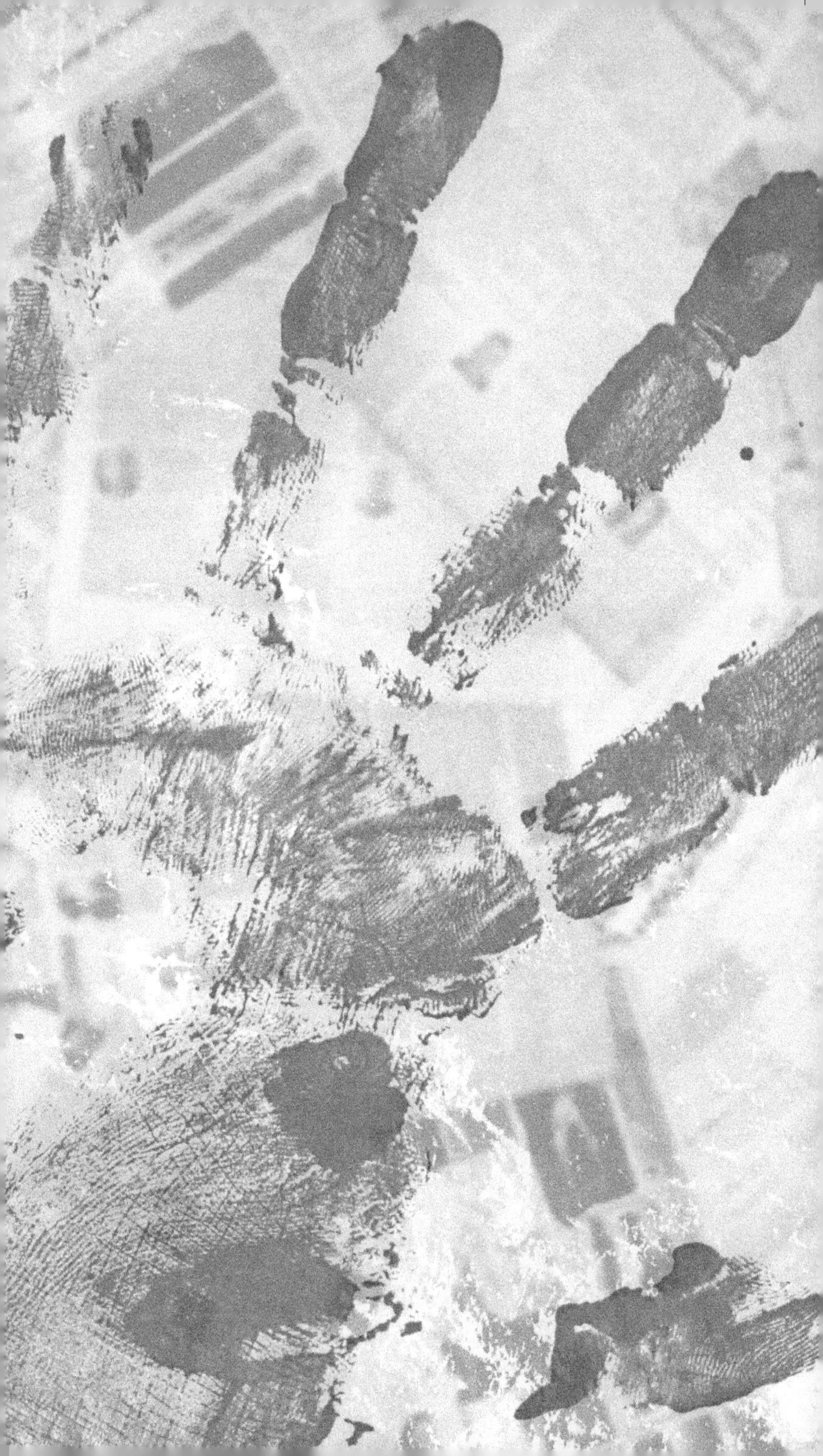

PRESENT DAY

He wrapped his hands around my throat, squeezing hard enough that spit welled in the back of it. I started choking. Caine's reach was long, and even from across the counter, he didn't seem to strain much. I wrapped my hands around each of his arms, pulling at him, but coming up short. His arms were so much longer than mine, and it took all of me to even touch his chest. Fingertips traced his body, his neck, his face.

My vision was blurring at the seams, and I could only imagine what he was looking at in return. Face purpled and bruised, lip torn and hanging there limply. I was not the woman he married. I pressed hard with the pads of my fingers against his cheeks, close to his eyes and heard him grunt.

Caine let go, and I felt myself falling towards the floor once again. He wasn't done with me, merely getting closer so that he could inflict more damage.

"You will not leave me," he threatened as he closed in. I watched him reach for my arm, pulling it up to his face so he could inspect the ring on it. Caine looked at my ring finger, and smiled as he snapped it in half.

I could only feel pain.

"I wonder if they'll cry for me, when you're gone."

Another snap of one of my other fingers sent me. I scrambled, pushing away from him and running from the kitchen. I needed to get to the front door.

I think he enjoyed the thrill of the chase. I could almost feel the light in his eyes when he pursued. He was a feline predator, hunting, stalking, watching me as I frantically pushed away furniture and maneuvered through the rooms of furnishings. I felt like I was moving through layers of water, each step was agony. I almost fell to my knees, and at times was only driven by the deepest desire to best him.

Caine's movements were more fluid than mine, how a man like him can look so graceful defies logic. He swept past each room as if it was nothing at all.

I thought I was going to make it.

Just a few more steps and I was going to do it. I was going to escape.

6 MONTHS AGO

THE KITCHEN SMELLED LIKE HEAVEN.

I wasn't a cook, that was all Caine, but on days like today I made sure my ass was in the kitchen with him. I was moral support, the trophy wife. I was best at doing that, being the wife he needed, when he wanted. That was what love meant, that was the type of love I wanted to give. It wasn't everyone's route in life, but it was mine.

I had so much respect for women that worked. People that found their calling in life early and went for it. I wished some days that my life took me in that direction. I wanted to go to college and have a career, at least when I was young. But then how would Caine survive here? Who would clean up after his messes? Being his wife was my full time job. I'd given up a lot to make him happy—and most days he made it worth it.

It was a pipe dream, working. As long as I was loyal to him, as long as I was an accomplice to his crimes, I would stay here. Marriage was a give and take, and if I left him now my mother would never forgive me. I would never forgive myself. I took long strides, went to the ends of Earth for the person I loved. Sometimes I wondered if I would be revered for that, and admired. Loyalty was a well regarded trait in this world.

Caine never complained about me being out of work, I think he liked the fact that he was taking care of me, to some extent. He worked a lot, and made a lot, and we were never wanting for more. I was happy, content with the quality of life we found ourselves in. And besides, it wasn't as if I did nothing. I tended to my greenhouse, I worked on the house. I gave him space, stayed out of *his* space. If he ever asked me to work, I would have obliged. But I was happy playing house like we had for so long. I think he was too, it helped us look normal.

God, I loved him.

His back was turned to me, and I admired the contours of his muscles through his plain white t-shirt. He was kneading dough, and with each flex I felt my heart drop lower and lower into my stomach.

"Are you staring?" There was amusement in his tone, and knowing. A small creep of a blush flooded my cheeks. I tapped my nails on the counter, proudly displaying that I'd kept them full and healthy for the first time in ages. Biting my nails had become my terrible habit, a way of avoiding and coping with copious amounts of stress.

"I might be, what's it to you?"

Caine turned around, one eyebrow raised, and it made us both laugh. He pointed at me with a flour-coated finger.

"Don't make me come over there," he warned. I saw through his threat, he knew I wanted nothing more. I skirted around our island and wrapped my arms around him. He was too big for me to connect my hands on the other side, but I could feel his warmth radiate from him. I wanted to capture it for myself.

"Do you want to help?"

I nodded fervently. Caine opened up one arm, creating a space between the counter and the bread dough he'd been kneading. "This is almost done, you shouldn't over knead your bread. You don't want it to get too tough." I slipped into his grip, feeling safe and protected.

He told me this almost every time we had a day like this. It didn't matter if I knew, or if he didn't realize I really did listen to everything he said. I loved hearing him say it. Every single time. Caine always was so passionate about the things he loved to do, and it was addicting. If only he kept this passion for things like this, and not just his knife fueled hobbies.

"I wish I could snap my fingers and have it ready." I sighed, replacing his hands on the dough.

"Where's the fun in that?" He argued, pressing his body firmly to mine. "You want to work for it, it's so much more satisfying that way."

My hands traced his arms, leaving a flour trail in their wake. I turned my head to kiss his collarbone. He groaned happily.

"Don't distract me, Sugar. You're going to start something you can't finish." he whispered, hands falling in the space above my waist.

"Who says I can't finish?" I argued, closing my eyes. He pulled himself from me, grabbing a pan from one of the cabinets above my head and lowering it to the counter beside me.

I grumbled in displeasure, which made him laugh again.

Caine sprayed the pan, then delicately pried my fingers off the dough. I helped none.

We've done this so often that I knew what came next,

and I walked to the sink, grabbing a towel and bringing it to him. He covered it and left it under the window.

"Caine, did you want—?" the question died as I faced him. He froze, pan still in hand, and I knew. I leaned in for a hug again, but it came too late. His body was still, his face frozen into a familiar frown. I didn't have to ask.

I was a good wife, I knew when my husband was distressed.

It was then that I heard it, and internally I cringed. I forgot that we'd had the television on in the other room. I could hear the news on in the background. This was when it was most dangerous for us, I think we both tried to forget the second lives we lived. It was times like these that snapped us back to reality.

The bread was now left proofing, forgotten. I would have to make a mental note to remember to check it. I walked into the living room, leaving him to gather himself. I had to remain oblivious, I had to pretend that nothing was amiss.

"I'm going to hang out on the couch for a second!" I yelled, knowing he wouldn't answer me. He didn't need to know that I was trying to help him. I was going to change the channel and we would forget this moment that never happened.

I searched for the remote on the couch, plopping myself down and digging my hands deep into the cushions.

"Don't change it." His tone was low, eerie. It made the blood inside me stop pumping. A chill fell over me, and my face contorted into fear. I was so glad he wasn't in here with me, I was forgetting my poker face.

"Oh, okay!" I managed to call back. I tried to smile but found that it shook more than I wanted it to.

"Another, missing. Killer, at large."

I only got bits and pieces of it, but I couldn't look away. I didn't even notice when Caine appeared right next to me. When he spoke I jumped, covering it with uncoordinated movements of my arms and a less-than-believable cough.

"I don't know why they think they're dead. People go missing all the time."

This was uncharted territory. We never talked about it, not like this. I wanted to curl into myself and never return. I wasn't prepared for this, I couldn't handle it.

"They might be," I hedged, noncommittal.

"There's no reason why they should think they're connected. Every woman is so different."

Except for the fact that they were all women. He would know, he picked them. He didn't understand why or how they were onto him. Were they? I listened more closely.

The newscasters didn't know what they were doing, that much was obvious. They weren't real reporters, just people with notecards to read. I wanted to scream at Caine, tell him that we were okay. But I couldn't. I wouldn't.

"Still, no bodies are found. The families of the missing women urge anyone with any information to contact authorities if they are able."

No chance.

"Why are they worrying people if they don't have any proof? That's why the media is incredibly damaging. They don't understand that they're putting a completely irrational fear on people who have nothing to worry about."

And they're making it much harder for you to choose your next victims, I thought.

"New to the case? Let's take a look at the missing women of... "

I already knew all the details, I didn't need to rehash them.

Over thirty women had gone missing here. That was his first mistake. Caine started, and then he just never stopped. He was smart enough to not touch the same neighborhoods so close together in a short time, at least. The kidnappings happened roughly every month and a half, over the course of several years. At first, they didn't realize they were connected. Those years were the best, when the media didn't catch on.

He really didn't have a type, I noticed. Some of the women were petite with pixie cuts, others with long hair and big bottoms. Hardly any of them looked like me, and if they did, I convinced myself it was only a coincidence.

It wasn't until he wasn't careful enough that they sniffed him out. I think Caine got a little cocky. Only two weeks separated those girls, not almost two months. And they were friends.

That was the beginning of the end.

We were getting closer to the end of our rope, I knew that. But I wanted to hold onto us for as long as I could.

"Maybe they're right." I heard myself whisper. Caine's face turned to me sharply. I regretted it instantly.

"What do you mean?"

"What if I'm next? What if it is the same person taking those girls?"

He ignored the latter question, though his focus was now entirely on me.

"You are not next." He said confidently. It was the assurance that rattled me.

"You don't know that."

"You are safe here. Safe with me, Dulcie. Nothing will change that."

"What if the families of those women told them the exact

same thing? And where are they now? They could be dead." Knowing their true outcome made this so much worse. I could feel the panic settling, its claws gripping me tightly and not letting me go. My breathing quickened and my heart was shattering my ribcage. My proclamation was making him angrier by the second. I could feel his hands curling into fists.

"They haven't found any bodies yet," he assured me through gritted teeth, "You are overreacting. They will find someone soon, alive."

His lies sent me further and further into my downward spiral. How could he say that, knowing what he knows? Doing what he did? I nodded anyway, still not willing to give up my secret. There was no way his knowing would make this any easier. That bastard.

How could he do this to me, to us?

"Okay, okay, you're right," I said between my pants.

He must think I'm so weak, so stupid. Nothing but a trophy wife who couldn't think for herself. And I allowed it to happen. I continued to allow it, with no intention of stopping anytime soon. Maybe he was right.

My heart was breaking. My resolve was breaking.

I was damn near sure that I was breaking.

"I have to go check the bread," he said suddenly. I nodded wordlessly, letting fresh tears roll from my eyes as he walked away from me. I hardly noticed as my hand moved on autopilot, grabbing the remote control and turning off the television in front of me. I didn't want to see their faces anymore—it made this so much more real.

We were not normal. We were not the couple from the magazines, the ones people talked about, and were envious of. That moment in the kitchen, moments like that were coming fewer and farther between. I continued to believe that we were more, that we could be something good again like we used to be.

We were so much more twisted than that. I didn't know how to dig us out of the hole Caine dug. I worried that it would be that way for the rest of my life. I couldn't reverse the damage that was done.

We didn't fit anymore, this wasn't working. Maybe at one point, a long time ago, but not now. Now we were no better than salt and vinegar. Too soured.

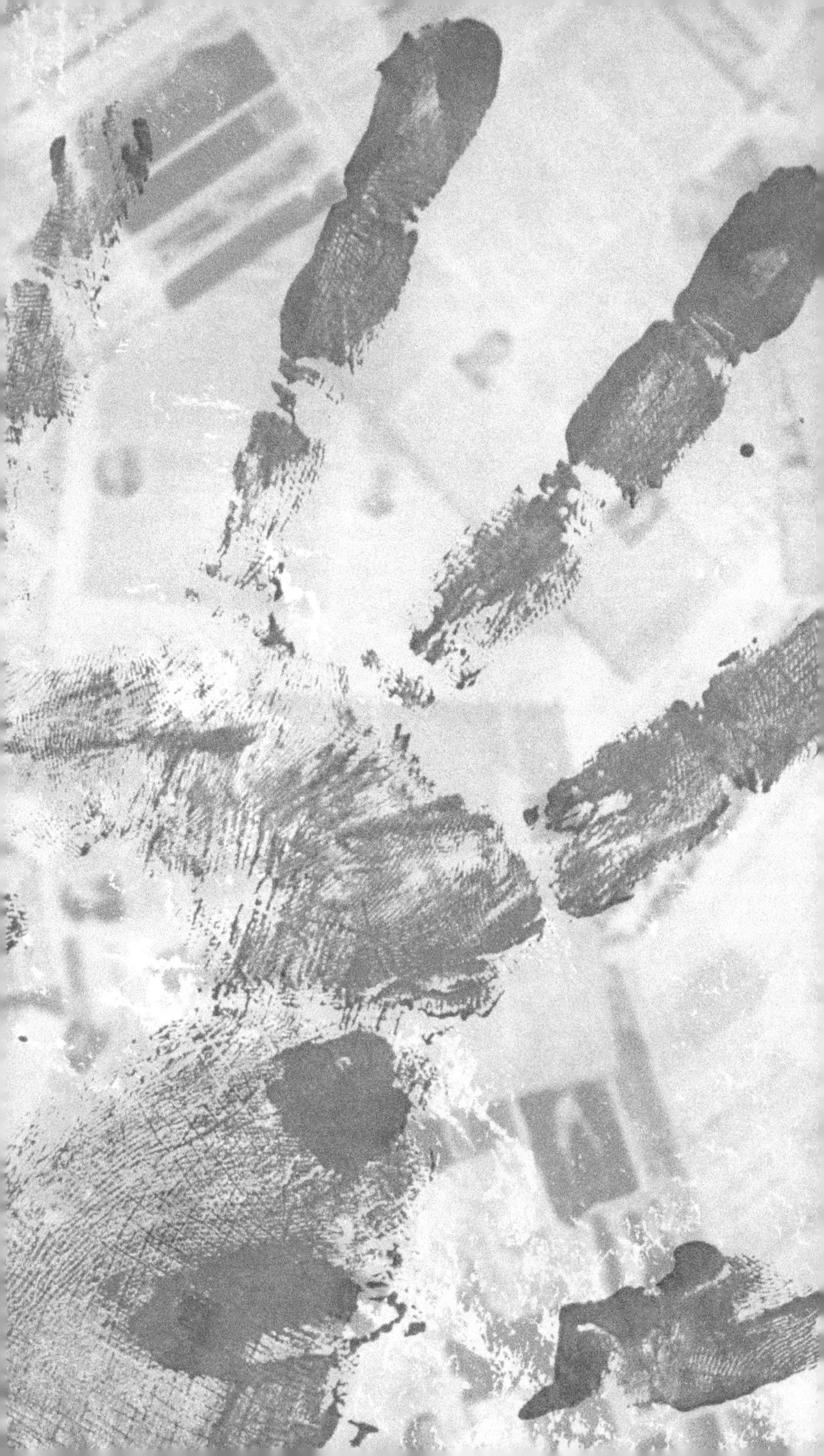

PRESENT DAY

I RE-AWOKE IN THE UTILITY SINK.

My hands, broken and limp at this point, were once again tied behind my back, the rawness of my skin burning against the rope. It was new rope, of course, not frayed like the ends of the last he cut me from. Caine was a smart monster, not the type to make the same mistake twice. This one was more bungee in texture, and even though I hadn't been awake to watch him tie me, I had the faintest recognition of it, like it might have been the same one I'd gone to get earlier in the week. I supplied his tools, and the identification caused an uncertain choke of laughter to escape. The irony was not lost on me.

He had tied the stretchy thing as tight as it was able and I felt as if I'd permanently dislocated my shoulders from the unrelenting pressure. It wouldn't be the harshest thing I've endured tonight, but it certainly wasn't comfortable in my current position. The utility sink was large enough to hold my entire body, much larger than it looked from my position in the chair, but I was folded in on myself and could feel the organs in my body shifting from having no space to breathe.

The cool metal met the back of my neck and every single inch of uncovered skin hurt with a sharpness that caused me to take another sharp inhale.

Caine at least did me a favor and allowed my legs to hang off the side, free-floating in the air even if I had no ability to move them on my own. I almost wished he was here so I could thank him for that small mercy.

He also left my mouth untouched, and the realization sent another wave of gratefulness washing through me. If only he could stop the dripping of the sink, which had only sped up, the pitter-patter sounds of liquid hitting cement an unrelenting force to be reckoned with.

Even without the rotting smell and taste of his sock shoved down my throat, I was still getting the rusted aftertaste of blood, metallic and tangy. So much blood—it was hard to keep track of where it all was coming from. Opening my mouth felt like I was trying to open a steel trap; even with the effort, it wouldn't budge an inch.

Everything felt impossible.

I don't know what he hit me with, but it was hard enough that I couldn't feel anything on my face anymore. Everything had felt tingly, and I was almost relieved to not be able to feel any pain at all, though the rational part of my brain that still functioned understood how dangerous an injury that caused that could look.

I couldn't move my head, so my eyes wandered lackadaisically over my body instead, soaking in everything they could. Every movement felt like it was going in slow motion, and I wasn't sure I was entirely there. My clothes were ripped and torn, but there was nothing to indicate how I looked underneath. Everything ached though, and I could see a bloodstream starting to puddle beneath me, so much so that it felt like it wasn't draining fast enough, or at all. The blood was coming from somewhere, and I had an aching suspicion that it was free-flowing from a wound I couldn't see somewhere under my clothes, and was assisted by whatever was happening to my head—the wound that was affecting my cognitive abilities. I realized now that the slow, steady pitter patter was the draining of my blood, and not just the residual water in the sink. I closed my eyes in resignation.

This was his messiest project to date, and it was one I'd be unable to clean up. I'd never gone to the basement while he was working, pretending to be asleep in our bed while he scratched that incessant need, but when Caine finally slid in under our duvet and slept soundly beside me—typically long after midnight struck—he was never soaked in grime or blood.

Sometimes I would stare at the basement door, tempted, but in the few times I'd actually been down there after knowing the horrors that took place, I would have never suspected that anything was out of the ordinary. It was weird, how someone so dirty could clean up so well. How unsuspecting he was until I knew.

I wouldn't say Caine was a chronic cleaner. He was, as I mentioned before, nothing but a seemingly normal husband, and person. He was the next-door neighbor that no one would ever question. The kind of guy you'd ask to pick up your kids or hold your bags as you used the restroom. So why was it I was sitting in a pool of my own blood? Why had he looked so ragged, so frantic as pieces of me were smeared across his smock?

Lost in my own thoughts, I couldn't hear him as he paced next to me, though I kept him in my periphery. Had he been there this whole time? Did I know that?

He said nothing for the longest time, and I assumed he

hadn't noticed that I was awake. A large part of me resented Caine for not killing me when I was under, or why he wasn't killing me now when I'd hardly feel it. Instead, he was waiting for me. Maybe, just maybe, I would allow that one thread of hope to snake its way back into my heart.

Maybe he didn't want me to die, after all.

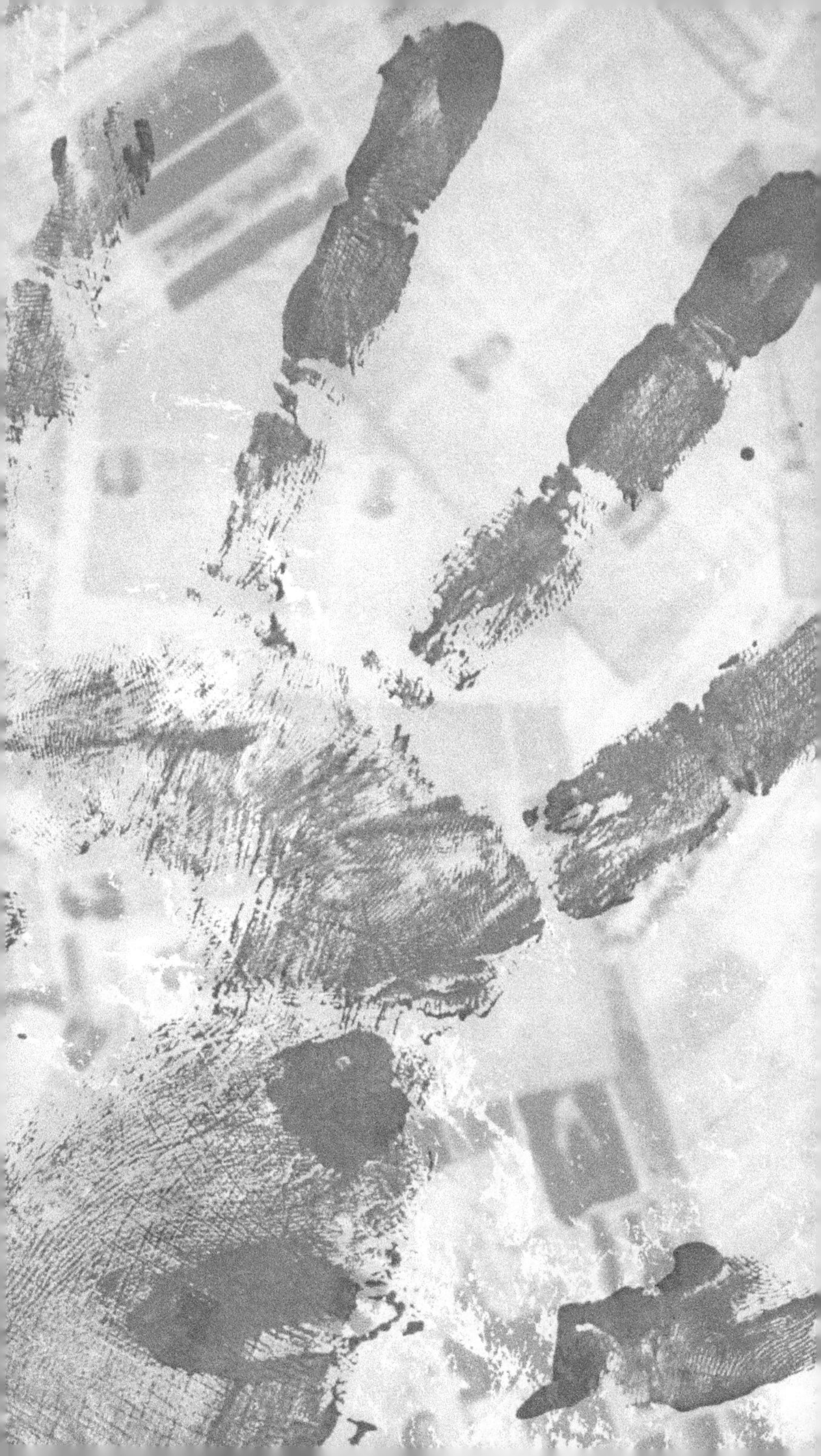

12 YEARS AGO

Caine loved driving. I think it's because it helped him feel like he was in control of something. That was okay by me, I didn't much mind being behind the wheel of a car. I was, instead, the keeper of the radio. He always let me choose the music, at least. His want for control didn't extend that far in this case. Which was good, because it made me feel like I had a grip on him; or, he just really didn't care for music. I liked to think it was the first.

His need to control might have been a flag for some, but it wasn't to me. I knew he had a rough childhood. It was the reason he wanted to go over to my parents so often. You clung to the normal you didn't have when you were young. I wouldn't call my family normal, but it was better than nothing. Better than what Caine had.

I didn't ask him too much about his past, we were still too fresh for those types of conversations. I knew he was going to be my husband, of course. I had chosen him the minute I laid eyes on him. Now I was just waiting for him to choose me back.

He could take his time, I wasn't going anywhere. When I picked something, I stuck to it. For better or worse.

"Could you lower it a bit?" He said, wincing. I nodded, turning the volume lower, and rolled down my window to scream the lyrics at the top of my lungs.

I knew it would make him laugh, that was why I did it. He shoved my shoulder, keeping one hand on the steering wheel.

"That, of course, is not what I meant, Sugar." He shook his head and blinked back a glorious smile. I loved when he called me that. He wasn't the first boyfriend I had that thought he was smart, playing games with my name. It was the first time I liked it, however. Maybe that was because every time he looked at me, he made me feel like the only person in the room. If I asked him to stop, he would. That was the difference.

He bent to me just as much as I bent to him.

My mother told me that those feelings would fade over time. That the honeymoon phase would disappear without us really realizing it, and we would be embarrassed that we loved each other as hard as we did. I had to remember that it was that way for them, that my mother and father were as far out of love as strangers could be.

I refused to believe that it would be us. Caine and I were different.

"Sorry," I laughed, rolling the window back up and reaching for his hand. He took it and interlocked our fingers on the center console, "I used to do that with my dad when we rode in his pickup out here. I love the country, it's so big and open."

"I like it out here too," He mused, using that moment to look around us. There were cotton fields everywhere. Homes out this way were few and far between. Most days I missed living out here. It made me feel a little wild, a little unhinged. I thrived here.

I knew Caine's plan was to move to a suburban neighborhood. He wanted the white picket fence and friendly neighbors. It wasn't exactly my dream, but as long as he was a part of it I would concede that one thing. He shouldn't get used to it, I wasn't the conceding type of girl.

Now wasn't the time to dig deep into his family trauma, and with that contemplating look on his face I guessed we were dangerously close. I wanted to keep it light.

"Have you ever picked cotton before?" I turned to him and watched as his sharp jawline twitched. He gave away nothing, no thought that I could decipher. I liked the mystery of Caine, I liked how he always kept me guessing.

One day, he'll be the golden retriever type of boy I sensed when I met him, with fewer walls and more trust in his face. He was just as afraid of getting hurt in this relationship as I was. It was scary when you jumped into the deep end with your person. I knew that he knew it, it would just take a little convincing and a lot of patience.

He shook his head.

"Not like this," he admitted. Our car moved over the patch of ground that crossed the concrete water drainage ditch, and up into the dirt driveway leading to my parent's home.

Mother, of course, was already standing outside. She waved at us enthusiastically. She liked Caine from the minute I brought him home, though I don't know if it was because he was him, or if it was because I was finally dating someone worth my time. Someone in it for the long haul. I could see her eagerness put him at ease, his grip on the wheel loosened, and he squeezed my hand before he let go to put the car in park.

I didn't ask him about much that went on in his life, but I knew from the little he told me that Caine's parents abandoned him when he was young. He has a few choice memories, but none of them were good.

I was glad we could give him some good family memories.

"Son, Daughter!" she yelled warmly, embracing Caine and I in a singular hug. I groaned in embarrassment, but I loved it. "Are you ready to get to work?" Caine nodded enthusiastically as I narrowed my eyes.

"We just got here!"

"And you're late!" she replied with equal force. I sighed, cast Caine an *I'm sorry* look, and we followed her inside.

I grew up in this house, and since I left it, nothing has changed. Everything was in the same spot—the only difference was photos I'd sent her over the years. She even put one up that had Caine in it. I wanted to point it out to him as we walked through the hallways, but he was in the middle of a conversation with mom.

"Aye!" I called her way, and I regretted it immediately as I watched her eyes narrow, her words practically skidding to a stop. "Donde esta papa?"

She looked between me and Caine, and spoke softly.

"Se esconde."

She made it sound so bad, but I assumed that meant he was upstairs. He didn't much like company, and he and Caine never hit it off the way I wanted. It wasn't a big loss, my father liked very few people, but I hoped nonetheless. Caine didn't seem bothered. My mother loved him enough for both of them. I honestly thought my father and Caine had too much in common. The only distinct difference was that Caine was nicer, and I was grateful for that.

We wandered into the backyard and my eyes widened in surprise. I forgot how massive the fields were.

My parents lived on acres of cotton fields, and I usually helped harvest them late in the year. Of course, as an adult my time was far more limited than it was when I was a child. They refused to do it without us, and so, we were a bit late in the year for it. The October winds kicked my ass, and I grimaced. Picking cotton in the cold took the fun out of it. My mother laughed at me as I wrapped my arms around myself, frowning at the chill in the air and the goosebumps now rising along my arms. Caine only smiled. He loved getting his hands a little dirty, in any type of weather.

"Everything as you remember it, mija?" my mother joked, only laughing harder as I glared her way.

"Honestly, I'm surprised you allow her to come out here," Caine interrupted, "she sort of kills whatever it is that she touches."

I rolled my eyes, storming away from the both of them and into the thick of the fields.

"It's cotton, it's not that hard!" I yelled, hearing them snicker from behind me.

Of course, I had forgotten my plastic bag, and my embarrassment flared again as I had to double back and grab it from my mother's open hand.

Picking cotton was a release for me. It was mindless work, and allowed me the time to think. I remembered loving it while I was young, and even in my late twenties, I found that I still loved it. The three of us worked for hours, and little to no conversation was needed. It was just nice being able to be with them, my family.

It was the first time Caine had ever done it, but he was a natural. It wasn't difficult, and I could tell as soon as he filled his first bag that he was having a good time. At some point my father even made it out to watch us. The closest I got to a smile from him was a lopsided grin, and even the chill in the air wasn't enough to dull our mood. In fact, it heightened it.

"Gracias por tu ayuda, mija" My mother exclaimed as she touched my shoulder, handing me a warm drink. I didn't realize how late it had gotten, and I blinked my thanks to her. I lifted the cup to my mouth and hummed in delight at the coffee that filled it.

"De nada, mama" I kissed her cheek.

"Let's get inside before it gets too cold." She shushed me —though the praise made her beam—and herded me like sheep to the kennel.

"Where are dad and Caine?" I asked, noticing their absence. How had I gone for so long without realizing Caine wasn't there? How long had he been gone?

"Your father took him to show him around the farm. To look at the tools, the cows, the sugarcane." There was something hidden in her voice, disappointment, maybe.

"Father took him on his own?" I was shocked, he never did anything without prompting. My mother shook her head.

"Caine got to asking him questions, and they went off. I didn't want to bother you—you seemed out in your own little world out there."

We sat on the couch and I curled into some blankets, looking at our spoils of cotton left near the sliding glass door. My mother followed my trail of vision.

"We did good work today. There's still some work for tomorrow, but I think I can convince your father to do it. You two are off the hook."

"Thank God," I teased.

My mother sipped on her own coffee and leaned back

in her chair. This was unlike her, the silence. She never stopped talking, fearing the loneliness that quiet brings. It was unusual in this home where music and voices were a common currency. I could feel a heaviness in the air settling around us as seconds turned to minutes. I watched her avoid my eyes, looking to anywhere else instead. She tapped her mug with long, painted nails. It was the only other indication that she was anxious, other than her sudden inability to speak. I'd never felt so much tension between my mother and I—so much that I was beginning to feel as if I was the problem.

"Where do you think dad took Caine?" It wasn't the right thing to ask, but I was beginning to feel more anxious every second he wasn't right next to me. Caine didn't know the extent of my father's secrets. He was hiding deep memories of his past from me, but he certainly didn't know the extent of my family traumas either. That father started beating my mother early in their marriage. That he would leave bruises so bigI would talk about them at school. I didn't think mother was weak for not leaving him, but it hurt me that she didn't feel like she deserved more than that. Or feel like she *could* leave.

Mother refused to answer. She did look at me, but it was a sad look, a lost one.

"Ma, are you ok?"

Her head dipped and I could have sworn that I saw a tear in eye. There was nothing more triggering to me than my mother's sorrow. I went to place my mug of coffee on the glass table and move closer to her, but she shook her head feverishly.

"Mija, mija, I'm alright," she whispered, though it sounded too close to shallow pants, "I promise. Your father...I just..."

I did go to her then, and wrapped my hands around her shoulders, bringing her forehead to my collarbone. I wasn't used to this, consoling the person who raised me. She was my protector, the strong one that kissed all my worries and pains away. I was not stronger than my mother, I could never be.

"I just hope to God Caine doesn't become him."

I knew he couldn't. Caine was good, Caine was innocent. He could never be the man my father was. He would pick me first, and always.

That's what you did when you found your soulmate.

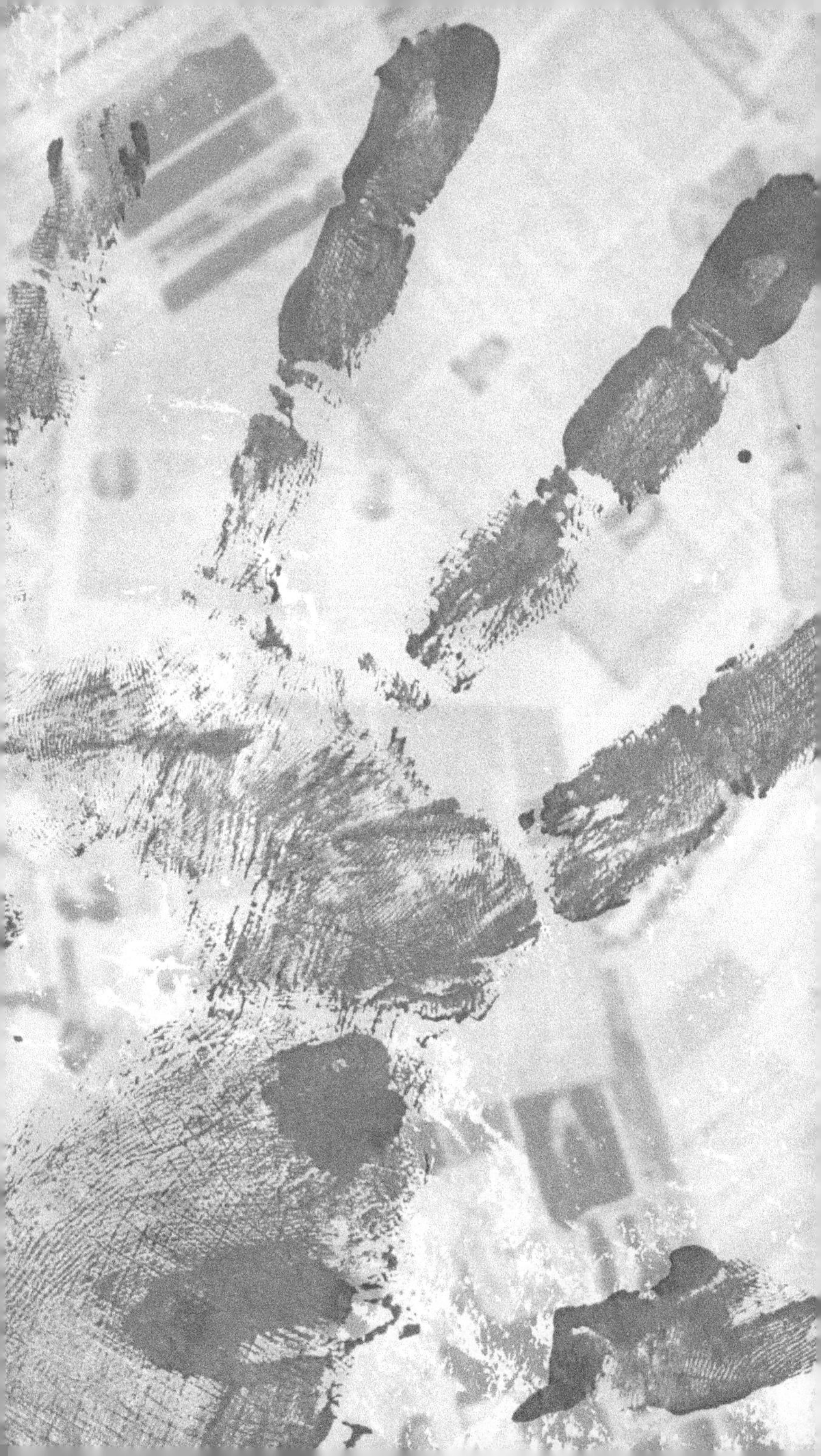

PRESENT DAY

I WAS NEVER FULLY CONSCIOUS AFTER THAT. I couldn't feel anything, and any type of sound that I emitted was nothing more than a grunt. Even my eyes had glazed over, and the focus continued to blur at the seams.

He noticed the flicker in my eyelids and I felt his movement stop. When he stopped, everything stopped.

"Are you awake?" He asked, almost sweetly, almost as if we were sitting on the couch and he was asking to take me to bed upstairs. He asked in the voice that I remembered from when we were dating. It was soft, innocent, and curious. I fell for it every time.

My mouth moved, but nothing came out. Instead, I tried to look at him. It didn't feel right, and every second spent felt like all the energy had been swept out from under me.

"Don't try to move, you'll hurt yourself."

Caine walked over to me and delicately touched the side of my head. He caressed it, poked at it, and when his hand moved away from my face seconds later, my blood came with it. I watched as he looked down at it. There was no fear, no regret. Just more curiosity. He reached into the sink to pick me up, and pain shot through me to my bones. There it was, the pain; the sharp sting of broken bones and open wounds.

I tried to scream. There was no other way the pain would exit my body than it would through fully agonized personifications of it.

He ignored my wails and dug his hands under my rear end to get a better grip, not even bothering to apologize as he lifted me and moved me to another hard, metallic surface.

My body was paralyzed to this spot, although I wasn't sure what I was lying on, or where he got it from. It seemed to manifest itself into existence, as if he pulled it from the shadows, waiting for me. I wondered if his other projects were given as much delicacy and care. I hoped so. Though a part of me resented him for touching another woman with so much softness, I was glad they'd left their lives being cared for. Prized.

Any ounce of me that was able to comprehend my surroundings had left long ago, and I wasn't coherent enough to interpret what was happening to me. What I did know was that the pain was gone again. My eyes fell onto him as he worked, spreading my legs wide and tying me to the table with long pieces of clear wrap. I don't know what he was thinking, I couldn't move even if I wanted to.

He hummed while he worked, a simple yet identifiable tune. I knew he was doing it to calm me down. Every time he moved I would catch a glimpse of his weapon. The cane machete had a blunt-tipped blade, and as he brought it down to my thighs I felt nothing but the finest bit of pressure. He pressed in deeply, sawing back and forth with the wide blade. The hook at the end caught on bone but he persisted, hacking at me until the entirety of my thigh separated from my body.

The world was dizzying as I fell in and out of consciousness.

"I nipped this from your father's house, one day when he was showing me around. I think it was early when we started dating, actually." He said out of nowhere, looking towards me as he awaited my response. I heard the thump of what was my leg falling into the bin he'd pulled up beside us. His cane moved to my other leg, this time starting at the knee.

There was more pressure.

"I loved going to the farm, and the fields. Thought it was weird at first, you know. We lived two completely different lives. I was the suburban boy, and you came from a family of farmers. He didn't like me very much. But I was fascinated."

My father, the man with wrinkles lining his face from years of sun and hard work. I knew he wasn't mistaken. It still surprised me, as they'd always been cordial, and my father never once warned me off of him.

My conversation with Caine was entirely one sided, my mouth tried to move to form the words I was thinking, but nothing came out. Still, he watched me with interest, knowing what it was that was going through my brain.

"I think he saw who I was."

That I wouldn't doubt either. There was another plop in the bin. I had lost the ability to focus on where his blade met and where it finished. He was deep into his work now, and with each sawing motion, my vision blackened.

"I tried to be who you needed. I tried to avoid this." Thump. Slice. Thump. "You looked at me like I was the fucking sun. But you know what, Dulcie? That changed a few years ago. I don't know what you saw, but there was a moment, a switch when I realized that you didn't orbit me like you had when we were younger. What did you see, Dulc? Before this last time?"

My mouth opened, but still nothing came out. Instead, the gurgled sounds of my choking on my own blood filled the room. It was just loud enough to mask the dripping from the utility sink.

"I think I always knew that you knew. You knew me too well. Or, at least, you thought you did. I started to believe it too. I remember counting down the days until I'd be sitting on our couch and the police would knock. I waited, but they never came."

The room quieted—the echoes of his confessions disappeared with the rest of my fading breaths.

"I pretended for a long time that you didn't know. But since that day, you haven't touched me. Not in the intimate, soft ways you used to. You avoided me. There was a part you played, ever the actress. You turned it on whenever we were around our friends and family. But when it was just you and me? You weren't that good."

I wasn't that good for my father either; I caught him frequently watching me from the corners of his eyes whenever we were around. That was always his way. Observant, but never one to intervene. He never directly said a word to me that caused worry, but he always embraced me in a long-lasting, overwhelming hug before we left him. He didn't start those hugs until I married Caine. It was a hug that made it seem like he would never get one again.

Caine's sawing moved up towards my torso now; I couldn't tell what was left of me. The only indication that I was dying was how far away Caine was beginning to sound.

Each time he opened his mouth to speak it sounded like he was down the far end of a tunnel.

"Did you let me become this because you loved me?" He asked me quietly. My non-answer was perfectly punctuated. "Was it worth it, in the end?"

I thought about that as he took another stab at my side. When my eyes flickered toward him, I noticed that my arm had been missing. The frayed edges of my skin and bone were enough to send me into another shock. The bin looked like it was ready to overflow. Blood caked his blade, his smock, his face.

I finally let myself close my eyes, giving Caine the permission he needed to finish me off. I knew I couldn't answer his question, not in the way he wanted. And so, I would let him enjoy his game, let him live out the part he was meant to play.

I was not afraid of Caine, or of what he did.

I was not afraid of dying.

I *was* afraid of the *after*; of the life he would live now that he wouldn't have me. I wished, as I had so many times before, that I didn't hide my secrets from him. I would tell him how foolish he'd been, and how sloppy. How, if it wasn't for me, he would rot in a cell, dressed in orange. How, if he continued on his bloody warpath without me, that future would still be possible.

I was afraid Caine wasn't going to survive without me.

My breathing stopped, the light finally leaving my eyes. I didn't get to hear his last words, the ones he kept talking at me even long after I stopped responding or understanding. The glint of the cane machete was the last thing that played in my head, refusing my light at the end of the tunnel.

There was no light, only blood, and darkness.

I think if given the choice, I would do it all over again.

Vol. 29

[REDACTED] News

Daily Report

MAN CHARGED WITH WIFE'S MURDER PLEADS GUILTY TO OVER 30 UNSOLVED MISSING PERSONS CASES

By: Anna Conroy

Caine Councill, 37, previously indicted by a grand jury three months ago for first-degree murder in the death of his wife, Dulcie Councill, pleads guilty to 33 unsolved missing persons cases, [redacted] Police Chief Gabriel Lake said today, in a press conference.

Now being coined as the "Sugarcane Killer" because of Councill's descriptions of his victim's killings with a sugarcane machete, [redacted] police will be searching for bodies in various dump sites located around the city, some of which have been missing for 5 years. Though none have been found as of yet, Chief Lake has stated that Councill provided details of the women that convinced investigators that his confession is genuine.

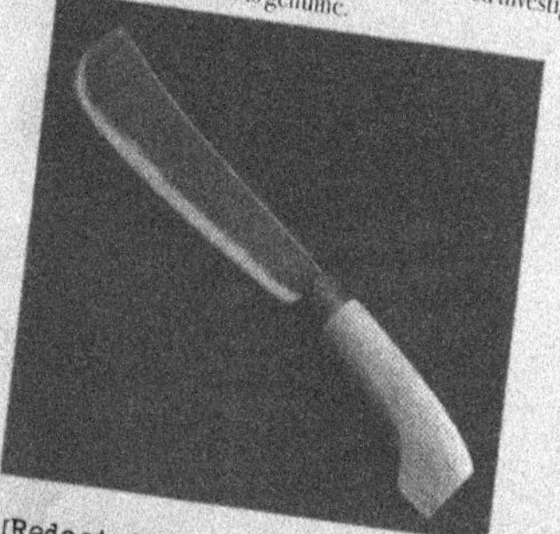

[Redacted] has been plagued with the disappearances of women within a forty-mile radius several times a year, with seemingly no connection other than their close vicinity. Officers have previously had no suspects, and Councill's confession might finally put an end to years of resident fears.

Neighbors say they didn't know the former construction worker's hidden identity.

"They were nice people," Marge Crout said to [redacted] News reporters. "My husband and I talked to them all the time. The wife was a gem, even if her fella' was quiet. We never suspected a thing!"

Councill blamed his parents for his upbringing, causing him to have a severe negative reaction towards women, he told officers. [Redacted] News reached out regarding the allegations, but has received no comment.

Dulcie Councill's body was found in their home after a concerned neighbor heard screaming from the house on their daily walk. Her father, Henry Mercado, says the death of his daughter has been heartbreaking and calls for the death penalty for his son-in-law.

"Justice must be brought to [him] for the pain he's caused me, my wife, and so many other families."

When officers arrived on the scene, Councill was arrested without a fight.

"Councill fooled a lot of people," Lake continued in his press conference, "he cleaned up after himself well for a lot of years. And now we got him."

Councill's court date will be next Sunday, when we expect he will be convicted for the death of [redacted]'s missing women.

PLAYLIST

- **Would've, Could've, Should've** - Taylor Swift
- **Sugar Cane (ft. Foster Olson)** - PrettyDeep
- **scare myself** - Nessa Barrett
- **Salt and Vinegar** - Light
- **Swan** - Willa
- **The Devil is a Gentleman** - Merci Raines
- **Panic Switch** - Silversun Pickups
- **You** - Greta Isaac
- **Leach** - BONES UK
- **Tear Me To Pieces** - Meg Myers
- **GOSSIP (ft. Tom Morello)** - Måneskin
- **Eat Your Young** - Hozier

ACKNOWLEDGMENTS

This is now the third book I've written acknowledgments for, and there are many days where I can't—and don't—believe that. What is even more unreal is how with each book, these pages of people look so different. I have been blessed with far too many wonderful people in my life, all of which I am so grateful for.

Each book comes with its own extraordinary amount of challenges, and the people I surround myself with have influenced not only my process of writing, but also what is within these pages. As I continue to find myself as a writer and an author, not only has my perspective on genre writing changed exponentially, but my voice and my passion too. *Sugarcane* was the product of me solidifying myself as an author in the genre I am wanting to pursue. Not only has it been one of the most difficult experiences of my life, but also the most rewarding. If *Stars and Other Monsters* was a dream, *Sugarcane* felt like coming home.

First and foremost, one of the most consistent and wonderful people I have in my life is my editor, and also one of my dearest friends, Alexis Aumagamanaia (@littlelionslibrary). You continue to watch and shape me into the person and author that I am. Your endless support and patience as I find my footing in this world has been critical to my development, and I know without a shadow of a doubt that my life is better with you in it. Your edits are always exactly what I need to hear—and are often completely unhinged—

but above your talent for creating, what I value most is your heart. I am so very lucky I found your corner of the internet.

To my lifeline, Tiffani. The world didn't know what it was doing when it brought us together, and it's been a circus of chaos ever since. You came into my life at such a crucial moment, and I thank every day where I get to keep you. Words are not enough to articulate how important you are to me. I love you to the sun and back, thank you for being one of my favorite people.

To my best friend, Katelyn. From the minute we met, it has been so effortlessly *easy*. To think we have lived so close, and acquaintances for two full years before meeting has been nothing short of an ERROR. I am grateful for all of our days together, for your support and feedback on my writing, and for just being you. You are such a good person, inside and out.

To the love of my life, Meg. I don't know why or how we clicked as fast as we did, but it meant everything to me. You are someone I always want to be around, and who I admire so much it hurts. You continue to be a big inspiration to me as I write, and I thank you for pushing me, and for supporting every wonderful adventure.

To one of the most talented people I know, Dani. I am grateful for *you*, period. You do everything for the people you love, without abandon, and I am so thankful that I found you. Your energy is contagious, and I adore every second of our friendship. A million thank you's will never be enough.

To my soulmate, Delta. Distance means nothing when I have you. To one of my longest-running friends, I knew from the moment we met that we were destined for one another. I am the person I am because of you, and I keep going because I know at the end of it all, you and I will never change. It will always be us against the world.

There are a million more people that I could thank, and not nearly enough time or space on paper. But additional thank you's to my writing discord, my Barnes & Noble 2866 team, my cover designer Ria @graphicescapest, my artist Pia @crimsonsdesigns, and to my early readers.

And thank you, reader. You are the reason I wrote this, after all.

ABOUT THE AUTHOR

Cassandra Celia (she/they) is a Maryland bookseller, turned author. She writes gothic, horror, and paranormal fiction, such as her debut, STARS AND OTHER MONSTERS, and her latest release, THE ELRIC UNDOING. Cassandra obsesses over stories with love, death, ambiguous endings, and everything in between. In her books, she takes inspiration from dark, haunting art and media, and she absolutely loves writing about angry, scorned women.

Stay up to date by visiting her website, www.cassandracelia.carrd.co.

facebook.com/authorcassandracelia
instagram.com/authorcassandracelia
tiktok.com/@authorcassandracelia